ZOE EVANS

CHEER!

CONFESSIONS OF A ₍Wannabe₎ CHEERLEADER

REVENGE of the TITAN

ILLUSTRATED BY BRIGETTE BARRAGER

Simon Spotlight
New York London Toronto Sydney New Delhi

This book is a work of fiction. Any references to historical events, real people, or real locales are used fictitiously. Other names, characters, places, and incidents are the product of the author's imagination, and any resemblance to actual events or locales or persons, living or dead, is entirely coincidental.

SIMON SPOTLIGHT

An imprint of Simon & Schuster Children's Publishing Division ✱ 1230 Avenue of the Americas, New York, New York 10020 ✱ Copyright © 2012 by Simon & Schuster, Inc. All rights reserved, including the right of reproduction in whole or in part in any form. SIMON SPOTLIGHT and colophon are registered trademarks of Simon & Schuster, Inc.

Text by Alexis Barad-Cutler

Designed by Bob Steimle

For information about special discounts for bulk purchases, please contact Simon & Schuster Special Sales at 1-866-506-1949 or business@simonandschuster.com.

Manufactured in the United States of America 0512 OFF

First Edition 10 9 8 7 6 5 4 3 2 1

ISBN 978-1-4424-4634-2 (pbk)

ISBN 978-1-4424-4635-9 (eBook)

Library of Congress Control Number 2012934727

Monday, A[...]

Morning in school, first day of freedom

Spirit Level:
Footloose and Fancy Free

Greetings, Dear Journal! At last, I have some time to MYSELF (for a change). This whole past week has been kind of a total waste. Dad and Business Beth spent the ENTIRE week here, "gathering their effects" as Beth likes to say, so they can "make their final transition to New York." In normal-person words, they're in the middle of moving. Whatevs, it was a giant snore-fest. Dad wanted to have one last week to "celebrate Port Angeles" (with me tagging along, of course), so I was busy visiting all of their favorite spots, from the diner in our town that serves amazing black-and-white milk shakes, to Panda Palace (de-lish lo mein), to the barftastic French place that Beth loves, Le French Frog (scene of much embarrassment for yours truly a while back, when I spit up the icky appetizer all over my mucho adorable new dress).

GIVE ME A
!!

This time, however, I was prepared: I wore a simple, cute, three-quarter-sleeve dress with a scoop neck that must be made out of some space-age material, because no matter what I spill on it, it always comes out.

Plus, there aren't any bows or anything that could end up being a nice bull's-eye for regurgitated food.

By the end of the week I had really had it up to HERE with eating out at fancy restaurants, going to local plays, and "shopping." I say this in quote marks because Beth and Dad tried to make it all, "Ooh, let's take Madison on a shopping spree." I was picturing something like the mall, or maybe even the very expensive but oh-so-cute Cecily's Attic (which I've still never been inside, I just like to drool on the window as I look in). But the reality was more like "Let's take Madison to snotty furniture and jewelry stores and occasionally ask, 'You sure you don't want anything?'"

Um. Yeah. I'll take one queen-size waterbed and a diamond bracelet that spells out "I (heart) cheer," thanks! Yeah, right.

The most boring day was when Beth got it into her head that she just wanted to "browse" at the jewelry store, Tiffany's. I think we clocked in at about three hours there, which in my mind is a little more than just

GIVE ME A 2!

browsing. I checked my phone a million times, texted Lanie a few SOS's, and even tried the fantasy route. I imagined myself as Audrey Hepburn in a little black dress and white gloves from the movie Breakfast at Tiffany's and practiced saying "dahling" as I walked through the store. And when that got old, I thought of the scene in Sweet Home Alabama, where Reese Witherspoon's fiancé takes her on a special midnight trip to Tiffany's so she can pick out her own ring (with me in place of Reese). That took all of five mental minutes, so finally I gave in and decided to see what was taking Dad and Beth so darn long.

I looked for the two of them where I'd left them at the necklaces, but they were nowhere to be found. I decided to try the third floor, where the elevator guy did his best at making a joke, announcing that we'd reached "Third floor, lingerie! Chuckle, chuckle."

And guess where I found them? Looking at RINGS. Rings! As in, engagement rings.

Couldn't they have done that in private? Why did I have to be involved? They didn't see me at first, so I had the joy of seeing Dad and Beth in "lovebird mode," all googly-eyed and giggly as Beth wiggled her newly adorned finger in front of Dad's face. She was blushing and saying, "Oh no. I'd never expect such

GIVE ME A 3!

an extravagant piece," but the look on her face was definitely, "But if you were to buy this for me, I wouldn't be that upset about it."

"Um, hey, guys," I said, tapping my fingers on the warm glass case that held the jewelry.

"Oh, hi, hon," said Dad. "Where ya been?"

"Oh, you know," I said. "Trying to add to my collection of diamond earrings. But the stuff here just isn't to my taste," I joked.

Beth and Dad looked at each other, silently exchanging words that probably had to do with me.

"Madison," said Beth, "I'd love to have your opinion," and then she quickly smiled at Dad.

She pointed to three rings resting on a piece of velvet. The saleslady who had been helping them gave me a brief smile as if to say, "I feel for ya, kid," then disappeared behind another counter, to give us privacy, I guess.

"Which of these do you like the best?" Beth asked, taking a few steps back so I could approach the counter.

They all looked fancy to me. And pretty too, I guess, if you're into flashy diamond-y things.

"They're all really nice," I said with effort. I looked at Dad, hoping he might take this opportunity to tell me why we were here, even though I knew already. It was

GIVE ME A 4!

really annoying how they were trying to pretend that this was just a casual shopping trip.

"But if you had to pick one," said Dad, pressing on, "which would it be?"

"Ummmmm." I decided to at least try to be helpful. If I was gonna have to stare at this sucker at snotty restaurants for the rest of my life, it might as well be one that I approved of. I pointed to the one that was shaped like a teardrop, with tiny little diamonds all along the sides.

"That one."

Beth beamed. Then she looked at Dad and did her best attempt at being modest. "Just good to know, right, honey?" And then she winked. Barf!

My phone buzzed with a text. Lanie. I decided to exit the scene of the crime and go skulk around a jewelry display that wasn't as likely to make me lose my breakfast (how's that for <u>Breakfast at Tiffany's</u>?).

"U hangin' in therrrr?"

"Ugh, barely. Looking @ engagement rings with D & B."

"Srsly?"

"Oh yeah."

"Duuuuuude. Srry."

"☹"

I felt a tap on my shoulder.

GIVE ME A 5!

"You ready to go?" asked Dad cheerfully. "I'm starving. How 'bout you?"

I shrugged. "Yeah, food sounds good." I could have been stuffed to the gills and I still would have agreed to get out of there. I felt like I was running from possible wedding bells as we finally made it out to the safety of the street.

Luckily, the week ended without a proposal (phew for now) and the lovebirds are back in their temporary apartment in New York. But unforch, all that quality time spent with Dabeth (that's my celebrity couple name for Dad and Beth) meant no time for the stuff I needed-slash-wanted to do.

I still can't believe that Dad is really moving to New York for good. I mean, I am super happy about his Fantastic New Job and all, but it really seemed to happen so fast. Also, I'm glad I decided not to go live with him. In fact, I can't believe I was even considering it! Must have been something in that New York water. There's so much I still want to do here, in Port Angeles! For one, there's the Get Up and Cheer! competition, which is less than a month away (!!!). And second, I want to see what's going on with this Evan-and-me thing.

Still weird to see the words "Evan" and "me" on the

GIVE ME A 6!

page. Even weirder is what's happening with us right now (read: not much). Ever since Evan reached out to hold my hand on our way back from school a couple of weeks ago, things have been kinda . . . off. Well, not like "off" in a totally awkward way. It is just weird because NOTHING like it has happened since (no hugs, no knees touching when we sit next to each other, NADA). Like the other day, Lanie had to do some work at the Daily Angeles, so it was just Evan and me (ha-ha, there it is again. EVAN AND ME. Still weird!) at lunch. A part of me was hoping he'd scoot his chair closer to mine, but there was, like, a mile between our two chairs.

I had been telling him how all my time was being sucked up by Dad and Beth—mainly just to distract him from the fact that I was internally swooning over how cute he looked that day. He was wearing a Teenage Mutant Ninja Turtles T-shirt that was probably a few sizes too small, and jeans with holes in the knees. Plus, an Evan-style blazer.

Something about the softness of the T-shirt just made me want to hug him. Of course, I couldn't. Not in front of the whole cafeteria, anyway.

"What's your plan for tonight?" he asked me, dipping his fries into the extra ketchup left over on my plate.

I rolled my eyes. "Quality time with Mom. She gets

GIVE ME A
7!

a little clingy after I spend a lot of time with Dad and Beth."

"Well, enjoy the bonding," he said, the corner of his mouth turning up in a sarcastic smile.

"What about you?" I asked.

Evan leaned back in his chair. "Dunno. Maybe I'll play some video games. Or do some sketching." He shrugged. "Just a normal weeknight for me."

I don't know why I was hoping he would ask me to do something (since we hadn't hung out after school since the hand-holding night), because I'd just finished telling him how busy I'd been all week with my dad and also about my plan with Mom. But still, I guess I would have liked him to suggest something, even if I wasn't available. Or say that he wished I were free to do something (because hey, it's the thought that counts, right?).

Ack! First bell. More later.

LATER THAT DAY, AFTER (A) GRIZZLY PRACTICE

Okay, so my team is in need of a major attitude adjustment. Just got back from practice, and STILL, after all these weeks, everyone's still peeved about Diane leaving our team for the Titans.

The biggest downside to Diane joining the Titans (besides the fact that we lost an excellent flier) was

GIVE ME AN 8!

definitely that everyone had to learn new moves to our routine for Get Up and Cheer! Once she'd left, we had to give most of the flying and tumbling to Katarina and Jacqui, and then we were also down one person in the choreography, so for the first few days people just kept on bumping into each other and stepping on each other's toes. It is getting better day by day, but we all still kind of feel like actors who've been told they have to play different roles and learn all new lines all of a sudden.

I know it was a little shady of Diane to talk all that smack about the Titans when she was trying to join the Grizzlies, and then to turn around and start waving her pom-poms for **THEIR TEAM.** But honestly, I can't blame her that much, because I practically almost did the same thing. And I get that people are mad that when she first joined the team, we had to change our routine for Get Up and Cheer! so that it included **HER,** and now that she's left, we have to change it **AGAIN.** But seriously, it is totally time to MoveOn.org on the Diane thing, I think.

Jared, unfortunately, does not agree.

Today the Titans started their practice a little earlier than usual. So the minute Diane entered the gym, Jared's eyes locked on her, and he basically didn't

GIVE ME A 9!

stop glaring at her all through practice. It got so bad that at one point, the rest of the team was scrambling into pyramid formation while Jared just stayed glued to his place, swiveling his head around to follow Diane with his gaze. If he had the ability to shoot laser beams from his eyes, I am pretty sure he would have.

"Hey, Jared, the team's over here," I shouted to him.

His eyes snapped over to me like a robot that had just gotten his switch turned on.

"What? Oh," he said, sounding mildly surprised to find himself in a gym among his teammates and not inside an action movie where the hero pursues the evil villain.

He hightailed it to where the rest of the team was busy assembling the bases before Katarina mounted them to do her scorpion. "Sorry, guys, sorry," he mumbled.

"You okay?" asked Tabitha Sue.

"Not really," mumbled Jared. "I just still can't believe the nerve of that girl. We wouldn't have had to learn a new pyramid sequence if she hadn't left, you know."

Tabitha Sue (and everyone else) knew exactly which "girl" Jared was talking about, because he hadn't stopped talking about "that traitor" (his words) since the day it happened.

"C'mon, Jared. You're sounding more like Clementine Prescott by the minute," said Tabitha Sue.

GIVE ME A
10!

Small footnote here: Tabitha Sue has reason to be slightly biased (in a good way) about Diane. It was, after all, because of Diane that Tabitha Sue ended up going to the Sunshine Dance with Diane's good friend Ricky. Ricky wouldn't have come to our practices if it weren't for Diane. Which means he wouldn't have had a chance to lay eyes on Tabitha Sue. And then, when both of them were too shy to say anything to one another, it was Diane who finally made the introductions.

"Come on, guys," said Katarina. "Who is caring so much about Diane in first place?"

"I sure don't," said Ian, getting into position to hoist Katarina up into the air.

"Guys!" said Jacqui. "Enough with the Negative Nancy talk. Let's not get riled up right when we're about to throw one of our teammates into the atmosphere, okay?" (She was exaggerating, of course. We weren't yet at the level where we'd catapult a flier more than a foot into the air, but it was a good point.) Ian was a strong guy, so who knew what would happen if he threw Katarina into the air with a bit too much force?

"All right, people, let's focus," I said. I knew Jacqui and I would have to give the team a little pep talk later. We had too much riding on the upcoming competition to lose face over a bad grudge. We'd been working toward

GIVE ME AN III!

competing in Get Up and Cheer! for months now.

The pyramid was a little shaky at first, but after a few retries, we finally got Katarina into her scorpion, and then into a clean dismount where the team caught her and then threw her up a little so she could land on the ground with a V for victory stance.

"Nice job, Grizzlies!" I said, clapping.

As everyone stretched out, I went over to Jacqui. "Do you think we should have a team talk about this Diane issue?" I asked her in a whisper.

Jacqui nodded solemnly. "For sure. It's nice when the team bands together for a cause, but all this negative energy can't be doing us any good."

"Yeah, it's not good if the team cause is hating someone," I agreed.

At the end of practice, we assembled the Grizzlies in a corner of the gym where the Titans wouldn't overhear us.

"Listen, people. Get Up and Cheer! is practically around the corner, and we have a lot of work to do," said Jacqui.

"We'd have LESS work if it weren't for Diane deserting the team, making us have to redo everything," said Jared indignantly.

"Yeah, Jared's right," grunted Matt.

GIVE ME A
12!

Jacqui gave Matt a look.

"I mean, whatever," he said, backpedaling. Ever since around the time of the Sunshine Dance, Matt had started being extra nice to Jacqui. He must have asked Jacqui a bazillion times to go with him, but she said no until she decided to bring TWO dates to the dance—Matt and Ian. Two ex-jocks and a cheer captain, now that was a sight.

"I know you guys are still mad about the Diane thing. But we can't afford to mess around during practices. We have to stay focused," Jacqui said.

"Eyes on the prize, guys," I added. "And don't forget we're cheering for the Bowling League next week."

"Yeah, like that's something to go nuts about," said Ian with a sneer.

"Can it, Ian," snapped Jacqui. "Besides, aren't you glad you don't have to dance around in front of your football buddies? I don't think anyone you know will be at Bowling League."

"Hey, give me a little credit," said Ian, pretending to be hurt. "I broke it down on the dance floor at the Sunshine Dance in front of everybody, remember?" He ran a hand through his gelled hair indignantly.

"Sorry, Ian," said Jacqui, who couldn't help but smile at the memory. "You're right. You did seem to enjoy that."

GIVE ME A
13!

"Probably a little too much," said Matt, jabbing his friend in the chest.

Just then, Jared cleared his throat and inched into the middle of our circle so he could address the group. He sighed dramatically and then made a point to stare each teammate in the face.

"Guys, I think we went a little off topic, hmm? Listen, I'm sorry I've been so hyped up about this thing with Diane. I'll try to take it down a notch."

Matt leaned over to give Jared an encouraging pat on the back. "That's the spirit, bro."

"Well, at least until after the competition," Jared said with a sly smile.

"Tomorrow we'll work on more of the dance parts of the routine," said Jacqui.

"Yeah, if we can remember who is doing what move," quipped Ian.

"Ian, you should stop with the negative being," chided Katarina.

"Katarina's right. We'll be great," I said with as much enthusiasm as possible. I didn't want the team to feel like they were up against giant odds. "We're almost there. We just need to work out some kinks, right, guys?"

"Right," echoed the team, with as much energy as a group of elderly people in a nursing home.

GIVE ME A 14!

"Um, with a little more pep, people?" said Jacqui.

"Right!" said the Grizzlies, with more gusto.

Well, at least that was a start.

Mom and I picked up a pizza on the way home because she wanted to "celebrate" the two of us finally getting to be together after my long week with Dabeth. I was famished. You work up quite an appetite doing all this cheer stuff.

After dinner I logged onto my v-chat, hoping maybe Evan would be around. I saw his screen name was active, but I wasn't about to be the one to call him first. Before all this weirdness we talked 24/7. Now, not so much. Ugh.

Okay, so I just gave in and sent him a quick message:

"Hey E, it's M. U therrrreee?"

Waiting. Waiting. Still no answer. ☹

GIVE ME A
15!

Friday, April 8

morning, after special assembly

Spirit Level:

Feeling I-N-S-P-I-R-E-D!

Well, it has been a **SPECIAL** morning (**NOT**) so far. Principal Gershon likes to call all unplanned assemblies "special," but I think that's exaggerating a little. I always get my hopes up when Principal G comes over the loudspeaker in class and announces a "special assembly," even though I know there's nothing all that special about it except the fact that it wasn't on the schedule in the first place. I know I'm not the only one who secretly prays that maybe this will be the assembly where Principal G says that there's no school for the rest of the day, or that the school is handing out gift certificates for the mall because we've been so good all year.

At least it's a chance for me and Lanes to catch up on the morning's gossip in between classes without having to worry about being late to the next one.

GIVE ME A
16!

Lanie and I always wait by the same picture in the hall outside assembly so we can score seats next to each other. It's this oil painting of a big boat coming into a dock, where fishermen are waiting to unload it.

But anyway, Lanes was already waiting under our painting impatiently by the time I got there with the rest of my classroom. The teachers always make us walk over as a class so no one sneaks away to go to the vending machines, or worse (dun-dun-duuuun!), walk into town.

"Girlfriend! How slow can you be?" Her arms were across her chest, and she was tapping her Doc Martens impatiently (as if she could REALLY convince me she was mad). I noticed that she seemed to have on extra eyeliner today. And that's really saying something!

"Sorry. Mr. Hobart made us get into single file, but the girls kept on clustering together to chat, so he made us go back to class and start all over. He said he didn't realize he had to teach us what straight lines were, considering we were learning geometry already."

Lanie uncrossed her arms and hooked one through my elbow. "Blah, blah, blah. Ms. Burger totally knows I ditched our group. I asked her if I could go to the bathroom, like, ten minutes ago, and I never came back."

"I'm sure she won't even notice," I said encouragingly.

GIVE ME A 17!

"BTW, what's with all the eyeliner?"

Lanie batted her lashes at me dramatically. "Just trying out a new style." She shrugged. "Marc said he always likes the way I do my eye makeup, so I thought I'd add a dash of something different to see if he notices the effort."

We found two seats toward the back of the auditorium, where we could whisper through the usual announcements and hopefully not get in trouble.

"Um, Marc notices your eye makeup?" I whispered.

"What's wrong with that?"

"Oh, nothing. But Evan wouldn't notice that kind of thing."

"Yeah, but that's Evan. You guys have been friends since the sandbox. You could probably get a mohawk and he'd think it was the same Maddy."

"Gee, thanks." I'd be happy if Evan ignored all my bad hair days, but I'd like to think that he does notice when I look cute. What, just because we're old friends, we supposedly become invisible to one another?

"I didn't mean it that way. I meant, he probably is used to the Maddy he knows. It's not a bad thing."

"Yeah, whatever."

I searched for Evan's mop-haired head in the sea of students in front of us. I knew he had

GIVE ME AN 18!

English around this time of the day on Fridays (no, I am not a stalker). I found Mr. Cooper standing in one of the aisles and scanned left and right before I found Evan. I hadn't seen him yet today, and couldn't help but wonder what adorable outfit he must be wearing. Of course, if you asked me last year what I thought about Evan's dress style, I would have responded with, "What style? You mean hand-me-down chic?" and then declared how he was in need of a major makeover. But now all that's changed. Now I think that the tiny flannel he wears with a mismatched T-shirt underneath are the cutest, and that his dirty old sneakers have that eighties throwback look (even though it is completely unintentional on his part).

"Hey, Mads. You need a napkin?" said Lanie.

"What? Why?"

"You're drooling."

If it wasn't Lanie who'd caught me staring, I would have blushed. But what's a BFF for if you can't just be yourself?

Principal Gershon tapped the mic at the podium to calm everyone down. No one really pays attention at the beginning of assemblies, because it's usually just announcements about food drives and upcoming holidays.

GIVE ME A
19!

But when Principal G does her "tap, tap" thing, we know we have to shut our traps or the assembly monitors will be on us like sharks.

"Quiet down, students, please," she said in her strangely baritone voice. "I have a very special announcement."

"Ooh, special," Lanie whispered.

"Spring is in the air, and you know what that means," she continued. "That's right! It's time for the annual Spring Fair!"

A couple of teachers clapped, and the kiss-up-y students followed their example. A couple of people hollered their appreciation. I don't get what the big deal is. The fair happens every year, but because Principal G likes to "surprise" us with the date of the fair, it becomes this big exciting thing (for some people).

The Spring Fair may sound like fun, but I think it really isn't. Why?

Reason Numero Uno: It takes place on a Saturday, which means we don't get a day off from school out of it.

Reason Numero Dos: Everyone has to participate in some aspect of the fair. Which means we're "working" on a Saturday instead of enjoying our freedom.

(Okay, I'm out of reasons, but I like making lists. ☺ ☺ ☺)

GIVE ME A 20!

Some of us like to call it the Spring Un-Fair, because full participation means that unless you're running a really fun booth, you could end up with a lame job like manning the Ferris wheel. Usually if you belong to a sports team or club, you can get something fun to do, but you have to submit it to the Fair committee for approval.

Principal G gave her audience a stern look. "I hope you can muster a little more enthusiasm than that, folks. And when I say full participation, I mean FULL PARTICIPATION." She cleared her throat. "Now last year, some of you, and you know who you are, signed up for things and didn't show up on the day of the fair."

A series of mock "boos" rang up from all around the auditorium.

"This year, we will be taking attendance at the fair. You are required to be there. If you're not, there will be repercussions."

If Principal G had a sound effects machine, you'd definitely hear "Dun-dun-duuun" for danger.

Everyone started talking at once, trying to claim partners for their booth ideas, or trying to get the attention of teammates so they could get their idea in for their team's booth. I knew I'd have to help with the Grizzly booth—whatever it would be—but I also wanted

GIVE ME A
2!!

to do something different with just Lanie.

As if she'd read my mind, Lanie tapped me on the shoulder and said sweetly, "Madison Hays, would you be my fair partner?"

"Hmm, let me think . . . ," I joked. "As long as we can do something fashion related."

"Your wish is my command," said Lanie.

Principal G tapped the mic once more. "Remember, those students who wish to be on the Fair Committee need to sign up by end of day today in my office. We'll announce the committee members tomorrow."

Lanie and I shared a look. "Ugh, Fair Committee? No thanks," I said. The kind of people who signed up for Fair Committee were the same kinds of kids who volunteered to be on school juries when a student did something wrong. Lanie and I call those kinds of kids "the Kiss-Up Crew."

Finally, Principal G left the podium, and we were dismissed. Lanes and I did our usual, and stayed in our seats until the last person in our row cleared.

"Speaking of kisses," said Lanie, "how are the two lovebirds these days? Any flirt-fests I've missed out on?"

"Lanes, first of all, you know I wouldn't act like that in front of you. And second, I wish! There's been absolutely zero flirting since the hand-holding event.

GIVE ME A 22!

zilch. In fact, we've hardly even hung out. Unless you count lunch in the caf. So I totally wouldn't call us lovebirds."

"Bummer," said Lanie. "What do you think the problem is?"

I shrugged. "I have no idea. But I have to keep reminding myself that I'm the one who's been super busy lately. So unless he got all romantic on me in the halls—which, let's face it, is so not Evan Andrews—there really have been no flirting opportunities."

"Yeah, sorry. I get a slight gag reflex when I picture Evan being romantic. Please tell me you'll never call each other stupid names like Mookie and Pookie."

"Lanes!"

"I'm just kidding. I'm only slightly weirded out by you guys having a mutual crush on each other. I'd probably be more bothered by it if I didn't have my own thing with Marc going on."

We waited for a couple of students to empty out of the auditorium before we followed the crowd.

"Yeah, back to Marc Derris, what's the latest with that?"

Lanie got a really dreamy look on her face. Definitely not her usual "don't even think of messing with me" look.

"Well, we're not official or anything yet. Obvs, you'd

GIVE ME A
23!

know if we were. But I know he totally is into me. Like, the other day, we had to do some research for these articles we're each working on. And we just sat side by side with our laptops, reading the interesting facts we'd each found, and at one point he squeezed my knee. It was so cute!"

I didn't have the heart to tell Lanie that the only "cute" part of the story she'd just told me was the knee squeezing. Um, yeah. In my book, a cute date does not include the words "research" or "facts." But to each her own, right? It was so Lanie.

Before we parted ways, we quickly talked about what our booth idea would be. Lanie thought it would be cool to have a make-your-own-headband booth—like the kind that people wear like a crown in an ironic, "going to an outdoor concert" kind of way. I thought that was a good idea, but it would take a while for people to braid the bands, and then decorate them. I suggested we do a design-your-own-T-shirt booth, where we'd buy the T-shirts and have a couple of suggested designs they could pick. Like different ways to chop them up and tie them—which wouldn't be too hard, and we wouldn't need as many supplies. Everyone would get to walk away with his or her own Lanie-Maddy creation!

"We could charge for the T-shirts, but the styling

GIVE ME A 24!

tips would be free. What do you think?" I asked.

"Sounds cool to me. As long as one of the designs includes safety pins and patches."

"Deal," I said.

I realized that maybe this Un-Fair might not be so bad after all. I love having new crafty projects to work on. And this one counts for school. Sweet!

When we looked at our watches, we realized that assembly had run for thirty minutes! That meant thirty minutes less of science to go to. Woot! (Doin' little victory dance.)

LATER THAT NIGHT, SITTING ON MY FRONT STEPS

My science class was done early because we'd been working on group projects, and since my partner and I are geniuses (ha-ha), we were done before everyone, so Mrs. Manheim let us out. Freedom! Okay, fine, so maybe it was my partner who was the expert on the earth's water cycle and not me, but still, I helped.

I decided to get to the gym early to practice some jumps. Since Titan tryouts were over, I haven't been busting my butt as much over the basic stuff that I tend to be a little wobbly on. The thing about being a good cheerleader is, you can never stop practicing the "easy stuff." You can always make a move go higher and

GIVE ME A 25!

look cleaner. I was walking over to the Grizzly mat, when I heard footsteps behind me. I knew who it was before I turned around, because the scent of coconuts and strawberries gave it away—the unmistakable aroma of Katie Parker.

People seem to always smile after Katie walks by, and I think it has something to do with the fresh and fruity scent she carries with her. I guess people get pretty jazzed over fruit bowls? I'm starting to wonder if I should find my own signature scent—something people would always associate with me (in a positive way, of course). Do they make a scent that screams "cutest fashion-designer-slash-cheerleader ever"?

"Oh, hey!" I said. "What are you doing here so early?"

Katie went to pick up one of the mats from the nearby pile. I bent down to help her drag it over to the Titan area.

"I'm making the Titans do some pretty advanced stuff later, so I'm setting up some extra cushioning. Also, I want to practice it myself, so I don't look like a loser."

"Um, yeah. Somehow I highly doubt that will happen," I said, plopping the mat down.

"What about you? You're here early too."

I sat down and started stretching my quads. "Just

GIVE ME A
26!

trying to keep up the good work ethic you encouraged in me when you were helping me train for Titan tryouts."

"Right on, Miss Hays," she said. "So, do you have any idea what you'll be doing for the fair?"

I sighed. "For the Grizzly booth? Not sure yet. I haven't spoken to the rest of the team about it. But I think Lanes and I are also gonna do our own thing. Something fashion related, I think."

Katie shook her head. "Well, I am all out of ideas. Which really stinks, because it usually falls on the captain to come up with the best ideas. Anyway, Clementine said she'd swing by to help brainstorm."

I couldn't help but grimace at the mention of Clementine Prescott's name. Ever since I decided not to join the Titans after all, she's been acting like more of a Mean Girl than ever. The other day, she and Hilary were in the girls' room when I was fixing my lip gloss, and Clem was all waving her hands in front of her face and saying, "Ew. Gross. Did someone eat the burrito bowl at lunch?" Then she made gagging noises, as Hilary laughed.

Of course, the bathroom smelled like it always did— like lemon disinfectant and, for some reason, dirty shoes.

GIVE ME A
27!

"Whatever, Clem. I just came in to put lip gloss on," I'd said. I don't know why I felt I needed to defend myself to her, but she has a way of getting to me. Besides, I could just imagine her running out of the bathroom and spreading a rumor that I had awful gas or something.

"GROSS lip gloss," Hilary had said.

"Yeah, poop flavored," Clem had cackled as she walked out the door. And just when the door was open so that anyone outside in the hall could hear, she yelled, "Smell ya later, Madison!"

Seriously, what are we? Third graders?

Katie must have noticed the look on my face just then because she said, "You look like you just swallowed a lemon."

"Oh, it's just . . ." I always felt badly about saying anything about Katie's BFF, but Katie and I are friendly enough (I hope) that I could tell her what was on my mind. "Clementine's been acting particularly, um, 'special' toward me, if you know what I mean."

Katie rolled her eyes like she wasn't surprised. "Oh, yeah. Clem gets in her moods sometimes. You just have to ignore whatever she says when she's like that."

Yeah right, like it's easy to ignore someone trying to spread rumors that you smell, I thought.

GIVE ME A 28!

"I guess," I said.

Just then, Clementine sauntered into the gym.

"Hey, girly," Clem said to Katie. Then she looked at me and didn't say anything. It was like I wasn't even there. Katie seemed to get the hint that we were now in Awkwardville, so she walked with Clem toward their side of the gym. I gave Katie a quick salute good-bye and could hear Clem say as they walked away, "Please tell me you were only talking to Madison about her massive BO problem."

I was glad when I heard Katie change the convo to the subject of the fair instead of agreeing with Clementine. That girl makes me so mad!!! I just wanted to say SOMETHING mean back to her, but Good Maddy made me take the high road, and I just continued stretching.

Also, Katie is STILL being mega secretive about her New York trip and her audition and seems to remind me, like, every five seconds just how on the DL that trip has to stay. She's told me a million times that no one can see us hanging together, or else they'd wonder how we became friends. Everywhere I turn it seems we have to "watch out" for someone (mainly Clementine) seeing us talking together.

But I had too much else to worry about to get

GIVE ME A 29!

wrapped up in Clem's attitude problem and Katie's **BIG SECRET**. Luckily, I stuck to my plan and practiced my jumps over and over until the team started trickling in.

"Hitting the mats early, are we?" asked Jacqui, pulling her sweatshirt over her head. Her dark curls stuck every which way from the static.

"Oh, you know," I said, out of breath from doing a hundred pikes in a row. "Just setting a good example for the team. Hey, do you know what you want to do for the Grizzly booth?"

Jacqui went into a perfect split and stretched her entire torso onto the floor. (I wish I was that flexible. Still working on it.) "No. I'm, like, brain-dead about it. I figured we'd ask the team for ideas when practice started."

"Good plan," I said.

After our warm-up, we sat the team in a circle to talk about booth ideas. I didn't expect Ian to be all gung ho about a school activity that didn't have to do with athletics, but he was the first to volunteer an idea.

"I was talking to some of my buddies from football today," he said. "And they kinda had a cool idea for our booth."

"OUR booth?" said Tabitha Sue. "What would they know about cheerleading?"

GIVE ME A 30!

Ian shook his head. "No, it's nothing like that. Basically they feel really bad about being such jerks to the Grizzlies. And they thought we pulled an amazing prank at the Sunshine Dance, with our surprise dance routine."

"Don't forget your impressive solo performance," said Matt, giving a dudelike head nod in Ian's direction.

Ian actually blushed a little. "Well, I think that did have something to do with it," he admitted. "Anyway, the team wanted to make up for it in some way, so a couple of the guys thought it would be fun to do a dunking booth."

"Um, fun for who?" said Jared, raising his hand. "Who exactly is getting dunked?"

"Calm down, little man," said Ian. "The jocks will be in the dunking booth. And THE GRIZZLIES will be the ones running the booth. It'll be hilarious!"

"Hmm. I LIKE it," said Tabitha Sue.

"I can get down with that," said Jared with a smile.

"Vat do you say?" said Katarina. "It vill be the tastiest of revenges?"

"Sweet revenge," Tabitha Sue and I said in unison.

"Of course, thees ees vat I said."

"Well, guys?" I said, looking around the circle. "Is this a plan?" I raised my eyebrows at Jacqui, since she'd

GIVE ME A 3!!

been relatively quiet during the convo. I had a feeling she probably wasn't all that thrilled with "revenge" being part of our booth.

"Listen, as long as the football team is game, and it was their idea in the first place, I don't have a problem with it."

"Woohoo!" said Jared excitedly. This was like a dream come true. Revenge of the Nerds style.

I asked the team if they would mind if I also did a booth with Lanie that day. "Of course I'll help with any preparations that need to be done for the Grizzly Dunking Booth," I said. "And if you don't want me to, I totally understand."

"I think we'll be A-OK," said Jacqui. "You should do your booth." Everyone else nodded in agreement. "Besides," Jacqui continued. "How hard can it be to dunk a couple of jocks in freezing-cold water?"

"Cool. Thanks, guys." I clapped my hands and got up off the mat, to signal that the "business affairs" part of our practice was over. "Okay, team. I say let's start from the top with the dance part of the routine first, all right?"

Everyone was starting to get in formation, when Jared shouted out, "Wait, you guys. Come here for a sec. I want to say something, but I don't want to

GIVE ME A
32!

shout it." He cast a nervous glance over to where Clem and Katie were practicing. Then he brought his voice down to a whisper. "I forgot to mention that I saw Clementine Prescott signing up for Fair Committee at the principal's office."

"Clementine?" I asked, nearly choking on her name. Fair Committee is usually for nerds and Goody Two-shoes, not popular cheerleaders who rule the school (or at least THINK that they do). I guess nothing should surprise me anymore. Now that Clem signed up, it must mean it's "cool." Sigh. You couldn't pay me enough to want to be in charge of the types of things like who wants to run what booth, and whether they actually show up. Talk about a logistical nightmare.

"Yeah, I was surprised too," said Jared. "She practically clawed her way through the crowd to be the first name on the list. Like it was a contest or something."

"EVERYTHING'S a contest for Clementine," said Jacqui with a smirk.

"Wait a minute," said Tabitha Sue, with her hands on her hips. "What I want to know is how, by the way, did you happen to see Clementine signing up for Fair Committee? Is there someone ELSE we know who's itching to be in charge?" she teased.

GIVE ME A 33!

Jared's cheeks turned red. "What?" he squeaked. "I happen to have a lot of school spirit, and I like fairs."

We worked on our dance moves for a while, until everyone completed one run-through without forgetting their parts. Oh, and we've added a few different things to the routine we'd created for the Sunshine Dance: We're going to start the routine with the more difficult tumbling moves so everyone's fresh at the beginning and has their strength. We also switched up some of the synchronized parts, so a couple of us will be doing a move and then a few seconds later, other people will echo that same move. Jacqui had a great idea that we should incorporate some moves from the new Beyoncé video to perform when that song comes on in the playlist. It looks awesome!

I really like the choreography and am **VERY** stoked that everything looks good even without Diane being part of it. I'm still a little worried about the stunt part of our sequence, though. We're kind of rough on our pyramid formations, and Katarina keeps messing up on her back handsprings for some reason, even though she's always been solid on those. Well, there's always something to worry about, right? Mom says she's not worried and that we're just where we need to be in terms of preparation for the competition. "Working out

GIVE ME A 34!

the kinks," as she says. "If you had it all figured out, you'd be doing things over and over and getting bored with it. A little nervousness and doubt is healthy." I guess she's the expert. She's been in more competitions than I can count!

When I got out of the locker rooms, I was surprised to see Evan waiting for me in his usual seat on the floor by the gym entrance. It had been a while since he'd waited for me post-practice, so I totally wasn't expecting it. If I had known, I might have brushed away the sweaty strands of hair that were clinging to the sides of my face and sprayed some Body Shop raspberry spritz to help mask the "eau de cheer practice." Oh well.

He almost didn't see me come out of the gym, he was so wrapped up in the comic book he was reading (big surprise). Just as I was about a sneaker away, he looked up at me and smiled.

"Well, well. Look what the cat dragged in," I said.

"Nice to see you, too," he joked.

He held his hand out to me, and at first I thought he was doing that because he wanted to hold my hand or something. Then I realized with a big duh that he just wanted me to help him off the floor. But when our fingers touched, I felt a spark of electricity—like

GIVE ME A
35!

when you've been walking on carpet and then you tap someone on the shoulder. Ouch! But in a good way. I think he felt it too (or at least I hope).

"Thanks," he said, wiping his hand on his ripped jeans.

"No prob," I said, all super casual. Like my heart WASN'T beating a thousand times a minute when I was around him. Did I mention that this is still super weird for me to feel this way about someone I used to play with in the sandbox?

"So . . ." He was scuffing his feet on the floor, as if he was nervous too. "I just thought I'd come by and see what you were up to after practice."

If I could have given him the words to say just then, they couldn't have been any more perfect. Finally! It looked like we'd have a chance to hang out again! ☺ ☺ ☺

"Oh, well, drat. I was going to watch The Voice on DVR with Mom, so . . ." That was my attempt at a joke, but it kinda fell flat. Evan looked disappointed and was like, "Okay, fine. Then another time."

"I was joking," I said, giving him a shove. "As exciting as sitting on the couch with Mom is, I think I'd rather hang out with you." As soon as I said it, I was embarrassed. I sounded like a love-struck puppy. Bad Madison! Bad!

GIVE ME A 36!

"Oh. Cool!" he said.

Well, at least he didn't notice.

I called Mom, who had stopped by Mr. D's office, and told her I wouldn't need a ride home tonight. Evan's mom was waiting outside when we got to the parking lot, and I just hoped she didn't mind a sweat-soaked, smelly cheerleader sitting in her backseat. She was cool about it, though: she didn't make me sit on a towel like I might have done if it were my car.

We ate a quick dinner with Mrs. Andrews and then went upstairs to check out the latest in SuperBoy Land. I took my usual perch on the side of his bed, as he rustled through a pile of doodles and notepads that never seemed to make their way off his desk.

"How do you find anything in there?" I asked, uncrumpling a piece of paper that I'd sat on by mistake.

He bent down to pick a pencil up off the floor and made a few quick strokes on his notepad, then put it aside. "Photographic memory, I guess."

"So you know where almost ANYTHING is in that pile?" I pointed to his war zone of a desk.

"The madness and chaos only adds to my genius," he said. His fingers landed on the edges of a small pile of doodles. "Aha! Just what I was looking for. See?"

"Whatever you say," I said. I knew I wasn't <u>Maid in</u>

GIVE ME A 37!

manhattan or anything, but at least I could see the bottom of my desk and my floor.

Evan pulled up a chair so he was facing me and handed me the sketches. He was bent over toward me in his seat so he could look on with me. I could feel his breath on the tops of my knees. As if he could tell, he cleared his throat and moved his chair back a little. I pretended not to notice any of it.

Okay, so here's what's happening in this latest installment of SuperBoy: Everyone's favorite laid-back crusader now has a sidekick named BestGirl. And she just happens to be a girl who looks a **TON** like yours truly—that is, if I sported a full spandex bodysuit and a mask.

She has wavy long hair and freckles. Coincidence? Not likely. But then again, I **ALWAYS** read more into things than I should. So anyway, the cool thing about BestGirl is that unlike SuperBoy, she's not, like, some ordinary gal who performs acts of courage and rescue while looking like a normal kid. BestGirl is always dressed for action, and the second she hears that SuperBoy needs help, she zooms in on a cute pink Razor scooter.

"It's just a character sketch for now," said Evan. "I'm still working on the story."

"It's cool. What do you think the story will be about?"

GIVE ME A 38!

Evan pursed his lips in thought. "I was thinking of spoofing on the Spring Fair thing and making Principal G this mean, tyrannical ruler of the school, who is making all the dorks in school do the worst jobs, like trash pickup and stuff. And all the 'cool kids' would be doing fun things, like running the rides and booths."

"Uh-huh." I nodded. "Sounds kind of like reality."

"And it gets worse and worse. Like, she makes them clean the school grounds with toothbrushes."

I giggled. "For some very sad reason, I can see that."

"So all the dorks are crying and asking for SuperBoy to help, but one of the popular kids has trapped him in the funhouse. That's when he calls for his backup: BestGirl."

"And what does BestGirl do to save the day?" I asked.

He drummed a pencil nervously against his thigh. "Like I said, still working on it," he admitted. Suddenly he perked up. "Hey, did you hear about these guys who dress as superheroes at night and actually fight crime and stuff in their towns?" he asked.

I shook my head no. "You're not getting any ideas, are you?" It was a good thing I thought he was so cute, otherwise I'd have to have a serious intervention on

GIVE ME A 39!

this superhero obsession of his.

He motioned for me to follow him to his computer, and we both perched on his desk chair, trying not to touch each other. Slightly awkward! I was just glad that we had our first get-together FINALLY, and that everything seems to be ALL GOOD.

GIVE ME A 40!

Monday, April 11

In the hallway, delaying the inevitable (next class)

Spirit Level:
Feeling slightly second-rate

Hooray, for the almost-end of a Monday school day. Ugh, Mondays are the worst, especially if the weekend was fun. And I had an awesome weekend. Lanes and I went to the mall to get inspiration for our T-shirt designs, and I scored an **UH-DORABLE** tank top that I'll rock as soon as it is warm out. It has braided straps that are halter-style, and the back is covered in lace. And it was **ON SALE**.

Lanes found another of those crownlike headbands she's been so into lately. It has tiny skulls in it. I guess it is sort of cute—but I warned her that if she's not careful, she might look like she belongs to some kind of witches' coven. Or like she went on a tiny mouse-killing rampage.

Jacqui came over on Sunday so we could choreograph some cheers for the Bowling League this

GIVE ME A 4!!

week. It actually wasn't that hard to come up with cheers that rhyme with "strike" and "bowl." Luckily, I have a little bowling know-how (thanks, Mom and Dad for our bowling outings when I was a kid), but Jacqui didn't know a thing. I even had to explain the difference between a spare and a strike. Here is my fave cheer:

WHAT DO WE LIKE?

A STRIKE! A STRIKE!

WHEN WE BOWL

HEADS WILL ROLL.

And when we say "roll," we'll have two people do somersaults on the ground.

This one is also cute—we found it online:

SEE THOSE PINS STANDING THERE?

KNOCK 'EM DOWN AND MAKE A SPARE!

Hopefully we'll have some space in the alley to cheer. If not, I guess we can just do regular sideline stuff. Supposedly this is one of the bigger tournaments for our school's league, so maybe there will be a crowd.

I spoke to E both nights via chat, and he was cute and flirty, which is GOOD, but it is still super hard to say what any of it means. Ack! Boys.

Okay, so that was the weekend. Now for what JUST HAPPENED today. It isn't a pretty story:

I was sitting in Mr. Hobart's class, about to

GIVE ME A
42!

get called to the board to help figure out what
"LN" equals, when Principal Gershon came over the
loudspeaker demanding everyone's attention. As
if a person could do anything BUT pay attention,
considering the screechy, extremely loud sound of our
PA system. You know how they say that kids have a
special ability to hear super-high-pitched sounds that
adults can't hear? I swear the PA system must have
something similar going on, because when it's on, I look
around me and every kid is cringing. The teachers
always look happy as clams, though. Conspiracy!

I went back to my seat (score for not having to
complete the equation after all) and did my best to
cover my eardrums.

"And now I am going to announce your new Spring
Fair Committee," said Principal G. Of course every other
word sounded like, "Screech! Screech! Scraaach!"

"As a reminder, these peer leaders will be in charge
of deciding booth assignments and keeping track of
each person's task the day of the fair. It is not an
easy job, so I encourage you all to be respectful of
their choices, even if they are not in your favor."

Principal G rattled off the list, and when she got
to Clementine's name, I swear I saw the girl sit up
straighter in her seat and stick her nose in the air.

GIVE ME A
43!

So what? She's on Fair Committee. It's not like she won some kind of popularity contest, right? This isn't the Kid's Choice Awards. **ANYONE** who wanted to sign up could have been on it. It is just so Clementine to make being on the Fair Committee some big deal.

I really think there's something fishy about Clem signing up to be on the Fair Committee. Clem only does things for Clem—and while most kids (i.e., the Kiss-Up Crew) sign up so they can earn extra points from teachers—there is **NO WAY** Clem is doing this to boost a grade. There has to be something more in it for her. I just can't figure out what.

I was starting to think that maybe I needed BestGirl to help me out here . . . .

Principal G wasn't finished with her announcement, though. "You will be submitting your booth choices this week to the Fair Committee members, upon which they will be reviewed for appropriateness and variety. Your leaders will make all final decisions. If there are any disputes, please see the Head Fair Leader, Clementine Prescott."

OMG. Clem? Head Fair Leader? Nothing about Clem's style is ever fair. Everyone in class turned to look at Clementine. Her hands were on her lap, and there was the most serene smile on her face. Like all was

GIVE ME A 44!

right in this world. She reminded me of one of those blissed-out Tibetan monks we learned about in social studies. We'd watched a video about this one monk who could spend ten hours contemplating a blade of grass. But Clem certainly is no monk (as if!).

Principal G waited a few beats for people to applaud for Clem. I saw Clem turn to look at Katie, who gave her a smile and a wink.

"If you would like to discuss a particular matter with me," Principal G continued, "my door is always open. Except when it's closed, ha-ha!" (That's her favorite joke.) The whole rest of class, Mr. Hobart could hardly get anyone to stop talking about their booth ideas and pitching them to Clementine, who just kept saying, "You know the rules. Sign up at Principal G's office." Eventually Mr. Hobart gave up trying to give us a lecture, and had us complete worksheets with partners.

On our way out of class, Katie and Clem started laughing and giggling together. Katie gave me the slightest of nods, but I knew she wouldn't want to talk to me in front of Clem.

Lanes and I met up later outside the principal's office to sign up our booth. (Jared said he'd sign the Grizzlies up for the dunking booth.) People were swarming the door with the sign-up sheet. You would

GIVE ME A 45!

have thought my dream came true and Principal G was giving out gift certificates to the mall!

Lanie and I shoved our way to the front—or at least, attempted to. Lanes was doing that thing where she pushes me forward through the crowd so I'm helpless, like, "Hey, it's not me pushing! It's the people behind me!" We're a good team like that. Just as we got to the front, I saw Katie finish writing her booth idea on the list. Suddenly, Clem was standing in front of the list, her hands cupped around her mouth like she was yelling out a cheer.

"Everyone!" she shouted. "Get in a straight and orderly line, or **NO ONE** will be allowed to sign up." Then she pointed at me and said, "You, back in line."

"Um, Clementine?" I said. "I was at the front of the line."

She narrowed her eyes at me. "What part of 'get into a line' do you not understand? You're **SUPPOSEDLY** a cheerleader. You should know what a line is."

"I **WAS** in line and I was at the front of it," I said angrily. Technically, there hadn't been any line to begin with, so I hadn't exactly been at the front of anything but a crowd. But still. I fought my way there.

She closed her eyes and shook her head. "All I see is an unruly crowd. And if you're not in a line, then you won't get to sign up."

GIVE ME A 46!

Katie stepped forward and put her hand on Clementine's shoulder. "Can't you just let her sign up? What's the big deal?"

Clem turned sharply toward her friend. "Did Principal G appoint YOU Head Fair Leader? I think not. These are the rules. Everyone's gotta follow 'em."

Katie looked at me and shrugged. "Sorry," she mouthed. Then, as soon as Clem stomped off to yell at someone else, she rushed up to me. "Afternoon? Our usual meeting spot?" she asked.

I nodded yes.

"Awesome. Cuz I have something to tell you but just not here." She quickly looked back at Clem, who I swear frowned in our direction for a second but then looked back at the poor kid she was yelling at.

Lanes was already waiting back in the line, looking like a vein in her head was about to burst.

We waited as patiently as we could for an extra ten minutes more than we would have had to if Clementine had just let us sign up when we were right by the sheet before. Like most people, we'd chosen to sign up at the end of lunch period. By the time we got to the sign-up sheet, we had less than two minutes to get to our next class! I was dying to know what Katie had to tell me that was so important we'd have to meet in our secret

GIVE ME A
47!

classroom (I know it is so dorky that I still call it that).

Later, when I walked into our meeting spot, she was sitting on one of the desks, furiously texting away. "Oh, good," she said, when she saw me in the doorway. "You're here!"

"Duh, of course! I've been on pins and needles, wondering what you had to tell me."

"Oh, sorry! I just didn't want, you know, Clem to hear us talking . . . ."

"Yeah, she's been giving me dirty looks whenever the two of us talk."

"I know, I saw," said Katie. "I think that that's just Clem being Clem. Maybe she's still pretty angry about your not joining the Titans after you got in and wouldn't understand why I would still talk to you."

"Yeah, I figured as much. So? What's the goss?"

Katie giggled. "Okay, so you will never believe who e-mailed me the other day."

"Um . . . I don't even have a clue." Katie and I were friendly, but we certainly didn't share any of the same friends at Port Angeles. We might as well have been on two different continents, that's how different her group of friends was from mine.

"C'mon! Guess!"

"Well, it wasn't Lanie. And I don't think you'd be this

GIVE ME A 48!

excited if Evan e-mailed you," I joked. Yeah, the two of them had gone to the dance together, but there obvs wasn't anything between them. (T.G!) That would be awful.

"Fine. Spoilsport. Remember that kid Luc from New York?"

Suddenly, my face felt hot. Ding-ding-ding! I remembered Luc—from the night we all hung out with Katie's ballet friends. He was totally adorable and really funny. And unless I'd completely hallucinated it (which wouldn't really surprise me), he was definitely flirting with me that night. Especially when he cornered me in the kitchen when everyone else was still in the den watching some movie.

"Yeah," I said, willing the redness to disappear from my face. "I remember. He was, um, nice."

"So anyway, he and his whole family are coming to Port Angeles to see his cousin's new baby or something, and he said he'd have some downtime. He asked if we could all hang out. The three of us."

"Really? He wants to hang?" I hadn't talked to him or thought about him really since the New York trip, so it was strange to think he'd go to all this effort to see us. I couldn't help but be a little excited to see him. But why is part of me also annoyed that he e-mailed

GIVE ME A 49!

Katie and not me? I don't really remember the two of them talking much that night. I know it is silly to care, because it's not like I'm crushing on Luc in the least (there's only so many crushes this girl can take). Gah! I'm just crazy.

"Yeah. So, what do you think? Should we plan something cool?"

I nodded. "Sounds fun. But 'cool' is the key word. We have to choose something a little out of the ordinary, I guess, to take him to."

"Yeah," she agreed. "He's a New Yorker. He probably doesn't want to hang at the Jumpin' Java. And also, we want to go somewhere where no one from school would see us."

I told her I'd brainstorm later that night and send her any ideas as soon as I had 'em.

And I definitely understood her point about needing to go somewhere where other kids from school wouldn't see us, but I couldn't help but feel that this whole secret friendship routine was starting to get a little old.

(MUCH LATER) THAT DAY, HIDING OUT IN MY ROOM

Ew. Just came home to find Mom and Mr. D (oh, excuse me, "Ed") hanging on the couch with a stack of DVDs in front of them, and Mr. D's arm was around

GIVE ME A 50!

Mom's shoulder. I had to will myself not to run over and remove it. Like, ahem, there's a DAUGHTER on the premises, guys. I mean, I'm slowly getting over the fact that my gym teacher and my mom are an "item," but if I can avoid witnessing them together, I am a much happier Madison. Better yet, I'd be cool if they made fewer public appearances together at my school. Having the two of them at the Sunshine Dance was SO EMBARRASSING. Everyone was asking me about it at school afterward, and luckily, I was quick on my feet and explained that they were just chaperoning together. And besides, who ELSE were they going to dance with? The cafeteria ladies?

But if they keep hanging out together at school and stuff, I'm going to start running out of excuses.

Mom turned toward where I stood in the hallway and flashed me her happy-as-a-clam smile. "Oh hi, Madington! We were just about to order a thin-crust pizza. What toppings are you in the mood for?"

I wanted to say, "Veggie pizza, hold the PDA!" but again, held back. "Veggie, extra sauce, please," I said, because I like my veggies. I'm like Popeye with pom-poms.

"Coming right up," said Mom, punching the numbers into her cell.

"Late practice, Madison?" asked Mr. Datner, while

GIVE ME A
5!!

keeping his eyes on whatever movie they were watching. Probably another eighties movie, because Mom practically doesn't watch anything else. (She calls it being "nostalgic." I call it living in the Stone Age.) And BTW, wasn't it obvious we didn't have practice? Hadn't he been hanging with Mom all afternoon (i.e., our coach)? Talk about trying to grasp at straws for small talk.

"Nah," I said. "No practice today." I shrugged. "Just went out with a friend."

"Good, good," said Mr. D with a sniff. I don't think he would have noticed if I'd said, "Went to coffee with a lion tamer."

Speaking of coffee, Evan had asked me earlier to go with him to Jumpin' Java after school. To make up for the sweaty mess I resembled on our last get-together, I decided to put in a little extra effort before meeting him on the steps outside of school. I borrowed some eyeliner from Lanes and fished out the handy-dandy face-blotting tissues Mom had given me from a trip to the mall a few weeks ago. Voilà! A fresh-faced, date-ready Madison.

Not that it ended up being a DEFINITE date or anything (for example, he didn't say it was a date). There was some flirting, but also lots of our usual weirdness. Like, I ordered my iced chai latte and Evan

GIVE ME A
52!

ordered his hot chocolate with extra whipped cream. And the barista was like, "Are you guys together?"

"No," I said quickly.

"Yes," he said at the same time.

Then Evan blushed and said, "I mean no."

The barista looked at us like, "Whoa. Not getting involved."

I don't blame her. Talk about confusing! How do you tell the difference between two people getting sugary drinks at the same time and two people going out on a date? Is it a date just because the other person asks you to go somewhere with them? Or is it a date when someone offers to pay for you? That time we went to Just Desserts was definitely a date, but that was more obvious because it was a special place that we'd never gone to before, and we both got dressed up. But Jumpin' Java was just a hangout spot. We've gone there a million times. Why isn't there a how-to manual on this stuff?

I quickly fished my cashola out of my purse so he wouldn't feel like he had to pay for me. The barista must have gotten the hint (T.G.) because she took it from me and rang up just my chai.

Drinks in hand, we found a spot at a smaller table toward the back.

GIVE ME A 53!

"So for the fair, I was thinking about doing a SuperBoy booth. What do you think?"

"Did you sign up already? Because if not, I'm sure Clementine will have some reason why late signer-uppers won't get the booths they want."

Evan shook his head. "I'm better than that. I signed up the other day."

"Cool." I took a big gulp of my chai. DELISH!

Evan cupped his mug between his hands and took a tentative lick of whipped cream from the top. A tiny bit of whipped cream clung to his upper lip, but I didn't have the heart to say anything. So cute!

"So as I was saying," he continued, "I could sell all the issues I have so far, and then I can offer to draw original SuperBoy sketches for all the fans."

"The fans?" I joked. "Do you have a secret fan club that I don't know about?"

Evan smiled. "Oh yeah. Groupies. Lots of 'em."

"Yeah, I'm so sure," I joked. "More like maybe me and your mom."

"Hey, that's harsh. But at least you're one of them." He looked at me for just a beat too long, and we both looked away and stared into our cups.

To change the subject, I told him about my booth idea with Lanie, and he said he thought it was cool too.

GIVE ME A 54!

"So what are the Grizzlies and the Titans doing?"

"Actually, I have no idea what those Titans are up to," I said, the realization hitting me as I said it. "I was talking to Katie about it the other day, but at that point she had no clue. I'm sure it won't be as fun as the Grizzly booth, though," I added with a laugh. "We're dunking the jocks."

Evan looked at me like I had two heads, so I explained how that all came about, and he was laughing so hard some hot chocolate came out of his nose.

But the subject of Katie almost made me mention Luc's visit. I was this close to telling Evan about how we had this friend coming to town and asking him if he knew of any "cool but not near school" places for us to all meet. Then I remembered that this whole thing is a secret and that I can't even tell one of my best friends about it. Because if I mentioned Luc, I'd have to mention how I met him, which would lead to me revealing Katie's trip to New York and the reason she was there, which were all out of the question (wow, that's a long explanation). So unfair! I don't like keeping things from Evan. But a part of me also wondered if Evan would be mad that I hadn't ever mentioned this Luc guy before and here he was all of a sudden, visiting me. (Again, the reason being that SOMEONE

GIVE ME A 55!

has a secret I have sworn to keep.) So maybe it's a good thing I can't tell him about my plans with Luc and Katie? I don't know . . . .

Before we knew it, Evan's dad was calling to say he was outside the coffee shop (he was picking us up on his way home from work). I felt like we'd been there for, like, ten minutes, but then I looked at my watch and it said it was seven thirty! Time flies when you're having fun. Or when you're on a date that's not necessarily a date.

So anyway, I've been looking up events and places (until the pizza delivery gets here) where we can take Luc. Here are some of the "best of" in and around Port Angeles. Don't get too excited:

Farmer's market. (Uh, baby carrots, anyone?)

Sardine tasting in the square. (Blech!)

Best of Bach Concert on the Grass. (Giant snore.)

Yeah. None of these would really work. I realized I'd have to get a little more creative. I decided to check out what's going on in the city, and found a really cool art gallery that's displaying the works of local street artists.

That sounds way more like Luc. And the best part? The gallery is also known for their ridiculously

GIVE ME A 56!

decadent desserts. Some of the reviews of the place said that the Death by Chocolate cake is an absolute must when you go there. I don't need much convincing when it comes to chocolate cake (hold the death, though).

Can someone spell Y-U-M?

Hopefully Katie will like the idea. Fingers crossed! Okay, pizza's here, gotta go chow down!

GIVE ME A 57!

Tuesday, April 12

Exiting the principal's office
(but it's not what you think!)

Spirit Level:

1-2-3-4, Feeling Just a Little Sore

Today was **THE DAY** when everyone would find
out whether their booths got the green light from
the Fair Committee. Lanes and I decided to meet as
soon as the lists were supposed to be posted. Last
night we'd talked until I was practically falling asleep
midsentence, thinking of cool designs for our T-shirts,
so we were more than ready to see if our booth made
the list.

When we got to Principal Gershon's office, she was
just finishing taping the sign to the door.

"Girls, right on time," she said. She raised an
eyebrow. "I hope you didn't leave any of your classes
early."

We both shook our heads. "Nope, we have study
hall now," said Lanie. Which was the truth. Luckily,
Principal G failed to point out that study hall meant

GIVE ME A
58!

we were supposed to actually be studying in the library. Oops!

"Well, all right," she said, scanning the list. She pointed to a line on the second page. "Madison, the Grizzly booth is right here. Right under the swim team's wedding booth."

"Thanks, Principal Gershon," I said, walking up to the list to inspect it myself. I knew the team would be psyched that their dunking booth was a go. I was going to ask her if she saw Lanie's and my booth listed, but she'd already gone into her office and picked up the phone.

"So?" said Lanie. "What about us?"

I kept looking. There were the Titans with their Fashion Faux Pas booth (whatever that means). I searched page three, then four, but still we weren't listed. Finally I got to the end:

"Earth Lovers Club: Adopt a Tree."

And that was it. No "Design a T" booth was listed at all. I couldn't believe we didn't make the cut!

"I am so doomed," said Lanie. "If I get stuck running the bumper cars rides, I'm going to have to kill someone."

Lanie was right. Anyone who wasn't running a booth would have to do some other fair-related task, like working at the babysitting center or directing cars at

GIVE ME A 59!

the school parking lot. Totally not fun jobs. Kids from out of town were known to throw things at people who had the really bad jobs, like cleanup (as if that couldn't be any worse), and of course there were the toddler meltdowns.

At least I had something to fall back on. Since I was part of the Grizzly booth, technically I'd be helping run that.

"But wait," I said. "What's the <u>Daily Angeles</u> doing?"

Lanie shook her head sadly. "Nothing. Everyone decided they'd rather have people reporting and gathering stories about the fair than have them waste time sitting at a booth. We're reporters—we like to be 'out in the field' as they say." She used air quotes so I'd know she thought that the school paper not having a booth was kind of stuck-up.

"This is a serious bummer," I said.

Lanes took a look at the list for herself. "I mean come ON," she said, banging her fist against a locker in frustration. "Even Kris Peckar got his 'Rare Insect Specimens' booth approved. What's the deal here?"

As if the universe was trying to give me a big HELLO, just then Clementine appeared from around the corner. I don't know why but I just have a feeling she had something to do with our idea

GIVE ME A 60!

not making the list. (Maybe that's why she signed up for Head Fair Leader.) She pretended not to see us and continued down the hall in the opposite direction.

"Hey, Clementine!" I shouted after her.

But she just kept going as if I didn't exist.

"Clementine!" I shouted a little louder this time, thinking maybe she just hadn't heard me the first time. I saw her flinch just a tiny bit, so I know she must have heard me, but she STILL kept on walking!!!

"Typical," said Lanie, shaking her head.

We stopped at the vending machines to get chocolate milk and orange soda. I needed a little pick-me-up.

Lanie took a giant gulp of milk. "So what do you think the Fashion Faux Pas thing that the Titans are doing is all about?"

"Good question," I said, stifling a burp from all the carbonation (because that would be mucho unladylike). "I can't exactly picture any of the Titans calling something that they're wearing a 'fashion faux pas.'"

It's practically a rule that every Titan dresses her best. And not surprisingly, that pretty much means they all dress the same when they're not

GIVE ME A 6!!

in cheer uniform (which I guess kind of puts them in a uniform anyway, but one of a different kind). A Titan girl usually wears tight jeans, a trendy shirt, expensive shoes, or a short girly dress or skirt.

Although, now that I think about it, sometimes Katie does her own thing and wears something that the other Titans typically wouldn't wear. Like the other week, I went to watch the Titans cheer for a home baseball game (also, Jacqui wanted to watch this uh-dorable baseball player who she's always thought was cute). After the game, Katie changed out of her uniform and was wearing one of those big floppy straw hats you usually see on the beach or by the pool. But she totally pulled it off. Seriously, I've never seen a Titan in a hat before. So of course, by the following week, the rest of the team had caught on and, like, five Titans wore floppy hats to school.

"Hmm," said Lanie, slurping the last sip or two of her milk. "Knowing them, they're probably just going to point out OTHER people's fashion mistakes."

I nodded. "That sounds more like it."

We still had some time to kill before our study period was over—and since we hadn't gotten in trouble yet for not actually being in the library, I figured

GIVE ME A 62!

there was no point in heading there then.

Lanie looked at her phone. "Hey, do you mind if I ditch you? Marc said he had a cool idea he wanted to run by me for the paper."

"Yeah, yeah. Just leave me for a boy and see if I care," I said.

"Maddy!" Lanie chided. "You know I'm not like that!"

"Just joshing. Go on, go see Loverboy."

Lanie sighed dramatically. "Yeah, yeah. Make fun all you want. . . ."

I went to the Lounge and found a cozy spot against the wall to write. I can't shake this feeling that something fishy is going on about us not getting our booth. Clementine has been acting so strange around me lately (I know, not like she's ever been my BFF or anything), so if she decided to mess with our booth idea, I would so not be surprised. I wonder if I should maybe try to talk to Katie about it first? Or would that be awkward? Katie never seems in the mood to say anything bad about her friend. I guess I understand. If the roles were reversed, and Katie complained to me about Lanie, I'd probably clam up too. But then again, Lanie would never do something to deliberately hurt someone else.

Okay, one more class before lunch. As Mom would say, later alligator! (Does anyone use that expression anymore?)

GIVE ME A 63!

THAT NIGHT, ABOUT TO PASS OUT FROM FOOD COMA

Confession: I just finished an entire pint of Ben & Jerry's Phish Food. I've taken out my frustration about the Spring Fair on ice cream! Uggghhh. Here's how the rest of the day played out: I kept trying to pin down Clementine about the booth thing, but she was like a clever ghost: I'd see her and she'd disappear around a corner before I had a chance to talk to her. I am pretty sure she was trying to avoid talking to me.

FINALLY, it was time for math class. (No, I wasn't rejoicing about the quiz we had that day. This was the one place I'd be able to corner the girl.)

I hustled to my usual seat and spotted Katie walking in as soon as I put my bag down. Which reminded me, I hadn't even told her my idea for the Luc visit yet. I'd been so wrapped up in my booth getting rejected, I hadn't even thought to tell her!

"Hey, Katie," I said, scooting into the empty seat next to her.

"Oh, Madison, I am dead meat." Katie had her bag open on her desk and was pulling out papers, pens, hair elastics, and various lip-gloss colors. "I can't find my notes for the quiz, and I didn't even study!" She put her perfect ponytailed head in her hands and breathed

GIVE ME A
64!

deeply in and out in frustration.

"It's just one quiz," I said, hoping to make her feel better.

"No, it's not," she said. "I failed my last two quizzes, and if I don't pass this one, my grade is going to go way down. I've just been so caught up in cheer season. We have, like, a million games one on top of another."

"I wish WE had that problem," I said, more to myself than to her. I know the Grizzlies would kill to cheer at another "real" game, like baseball, lacrosse, or even track. Lately we'd still just had Grizzly-type games to cheer at (think Math League, Chess League, Debate Team, and now, Bowling League). And as exciting as it is to watch a group of nerds scratch their heads over where their knight should go, we'd all rather be on the field with the athletes instead of the mathletes.

I ran to my desk and pulled out the study sheet I'd put together last night. "Here," I said, unfolding it on her desk. "Just take a quick look, and this should about cover it."

Katie looked up at me gratefully. "Thanks, Madison."

"Hey, and after class I want to tell you about my idea for when Luc is in town, K?"

Katie's face seemed to instantly perk up. I saw her look toward the door, probably to make sure Clem hadn't

GIVE ME A 65!

come in yet. "Oh, tell me quick?"

"Okay," I said. "I found this really cool art gallery in the city that is also like a lounge. They're showing some street art stuff."

"Street art?"

"Yeah, like graffiti artists that I guess are being seen as, like, real artists or something. Plus they have amazing desserts."

"Sounds familiar," she said. "I feel like maybe I read about it somewhere." She bit her lip as if trying to remember how she'd heard of the place. "Eh, can't remember. But yeah, that sounds like an awesome idea."

"Cool," I said, satisfied that I was the one to come up with the go-to plan. "So, next Saturday?"

"Sounds perfect. Thanks, Madison, you're really saving the day today," she said. Just then the smile was wiped from her face. "I, uh, gotta take a look at this before Mr. Hobart starts class."

"Yeah, sure, of course," I said. As I walked back to my seat, I saw the reason Katie got all hush-hush all of a sudden. Clementine had just entered the building. Now was my chance.

"Clementine," I said, as she passed my seat.

She turned to me and put her finger to her lips. "Shhh, Madison. A little respect? Mr. H is about to start

GIVE ME A 66!

class." She smiled at her own cleverness, gave an air kiss to Katie, and settled in her seat. Grrrr!

I quickly texted Lanes: "Can't get hold of Clem. Impossible!"

To top off this FANTASTIC (totally being sarcastic here) day, Grizzly practice was super intense. We had to go over our cheers for the Bowling League, PLUS work on everything for Get Up and Cheer! People were still getting confused about the timing of the synchronized parts of our competition routine. Like, Tabitha Sue and Katarina were supposed to go to the floor while Jacqui, Jared, and I did cartwheels and round-offs across the stage and Ian and Matt did hand motions. Then Tabitha Sue and Katarina were supposed to transition into hand motions while the three of us did the floor sequence. For some reason, both Tabitha Sue and Katarina started doing the tumbling motions instead, completely knocking the sequence out of whack! Also, no matter how many times Jacqui and I told Matt and Ian to make sure not to bend their wrists during hand motions, they kept slipping.

"Sharp movements, guys! Make those broken Ts snap!" I kept yelling.

"One more time, starting with hands on hips and

GIVE ME A 67!

eyes on the crowd," Jacqui kept saying every time we started over.

So we were stuck practicing that one part over and over and over. By the time we were done running through the routine a million times, people were bumping into each other and tripping over their own feet from exhaustion (and probably confusion). Even worse, they all started to complain a lot more.

In the middle of our hundredth run-through, Tabitha Sue, sweating buckets, just collapsed right onto the floor. "I stink!" she exclaimed. "I can't do this!"

"Tabitha Sue, of course you can," said Jacqui.

She shook her head, tears welling up in her eyes (Tabitha Sue has a flair for being overly dramatic at times). "No, I've practiced and practiced, and I STILL can't get it right! And the competition is practically any day now!"

"We'll be fine, Tabitha Sue," I said. "We have a few more weeks before the big day."

"I'm feeling pretty doomed too," said Jared. "We're gonna make fools of ourselves out there."

"Hey, hey, people!" said Ian. "I think we need a group huddle."

"Yeah, bro!" said Matt exuberantly.

Jacqui and I looked at each other like, "Huh? What is

GIVE ME A 68!

happening?" because WE'RE usually the ones to start the pep talks.

Matt helped usher everyone into a huddle. "Okay, so this is something Ian and I always did with the football guys when we were feeling psyched out of a game."

Ian smiled knowingly. "Jared, how much are you dying to show your drama friends that there's more to you than just musical dance routines? That you can somersault with the best of them?"

The corners of Jared's mouth curved into a smile. "Well, yeah. Of course I want to do all that."

Next, Ian locked eyes on Katarina. "Katarina, tell me you're not super hungry to nail that scorpion when you're on top of the pyramid?"

"Erm, hungry?" said a confused-looking Katarina. "I just had the snack, right before the practice."

Matt shook his head. "Sorry, that was slang. I mean, don't you want to get that scorpion perfect?"

Katarina laughed at her misunderstanding. "Of course!"

Next it was Tabitha Sue's turn. Ian looked her straight in the eye. "Tabitha Sue, how badly do you want to show the school that you've got moves?"

"You have no idea," said Tabitha Sue intensely.

"All right," said Matt. "We all want this bad, right?"

GIVE ME A 69!

"Yeah," said the team in response.

"That didn't sound like you wanted it," teased Ian.

"YEAH!" we all shouted.

"Louder!"

"Yeah!"

"All right!" said Matt and Ian at the same time.

I looked around our huddle and saw smiles on everyone's faces. Who knew? The football team psych-up worked. Jacqui and I think that maybe the reaction they got from their old teammates after they did their break-dance routine at the Sunshine Dance had something to do with it. Whatever the reason, I could get used to this new version of the Testosterone Twins. (Guess testosterone comes in handy sometimes!)

The one other good thing is that Jared seems to have calmed down about Diane. He seems to be less focused on shooting laser-beam eyes at her and more focused on getting the routine right.

It also helped that the Titans haven't been in the gym at the same time as us lately because of all their games. Thank goodness for small miracles!

I'm trying not to look at today as a setback, even though people's spirits were down. If I focus on the positive—the pep talk from Ian and Matt,

GIVE ME A
70!

the improvement in Jared's Diane-hating mission—
then I guess things aren't so bad. It is hard to feel
completely upbeat, though, because I'm still REALLY
ANGRY at Clementine.

I FINALLY was able to talk to her for five
seconds without having her ignore me.

After practice, when the Titans were sauntering
into the gym on their usual high horses, I spotted
Clementine walking with Katie and made a beeline toward
her. She must have realized she was cornered. In the
middle of the ginormous gym, there were no hallways to
disappear behind, and no classes to run off to.

"Hey, Clementine," I said.

She looked at me as if I were a bug that had flown
in front of her face—something she could shoo away.
"Yeah? What do you want?" she said, arching an eyebrow.

"I want to talk to you about the booth Lanie and I
tried to propose for the fair."

She examined one of the friendship bracelets on her
wrist, giving me the clear signal that she was B-O-R-E-D. "So?
What ABOUT your booth?" she asked. Then she cocked her
head at me like she was waiting for ME to explain to HER
what happened. Or like she didn't know already that we'd been
mysteriously left off the list.

I decided to hold the attitude and just state the

GIVE ME A
7!!

facts. "Somehow our booth didn't make the cut. I was wondering why."

Clementine let out a deep sigh. "I seriously do not have time to talk about this right now. You know we have another big baseball game coming up. Katie, shall we?" She held out her elbow for Katie to latch on to.

Katie, meanwhile, had become conspicuously silent during Clementine's and my exchange. I guess she felt awkward.

"Clementine," I said with a little more force than I meant to.

She whipped her head around to look at me, a sly smile playing on her lips.

"It shouldn't take THAT long to explain," I said. "I'm sure you have a whole long list of reasons. But can you just let me know what they are?"

Katie started pretending to fix the timer on her watch.

"Fine. Here's the deal," Clementine said. "The Titans have a killer booth this year. My mom, who as you probably already know is THE fashion advice guru for Channel 31, is going to be giving tips to the, um"—she paused to give me a quick once-over—"fashion deficient. People will come to our booth to get fashion advice, and a mini styling sesh."

GIVE ME A 72!

"All right, so what does that have to do with Lanie's and my booth idea?"

Clementine rolled her eyes. "Everything. We can't have two fashion-related booths at the fair, let alone two cheerleader-run booths. Didn't you hear Principal Gershon say we needed a VARIETY of booths?"

"Actually, no I didn't." I was pretty sure Clementine had made that little line up on the spot.

"Well, pay attention next time," she snapped. "So anyway, like, EVERYONE voted on our booth idea over yours. You were insanely outvoted. Plus, isn't it obvs? Everyone knows my mom, and seriously, who do you think they'd rather get fashion advice from? A famous TV personality? Or, um . . ." Her eyes went down to my fairly beat-up New Balances as she snickered. "Well, YOU know."

Finally, Katie stepped in and said something. "Clem, don't you think the booths sound different enough?" I could tell she was trying to sound all whatever about it, like she didn't care either way but wanted to add her two cents. "One is fashion advice and the other is fashion DESIGN. Those are two separate things. Who cares if they have a fashion-related booth?"

"It's not up to just me," Clementine snapped. "Like I said, there was a vote fair and square and the Titan

GIVE ME A 73!

booth won. Besides, what do YOU care?" she challenged. She didn't even wait for Katie to say something back. "Madison, look. You win some and you lose some. And honestly, of all people, you should be familiar with the LOSING part, right?"

Katie looked like she wanted to say something but was holding herself back. I could tell she wasn't going to keep defending me, which was a bummer. I liked hearing her talk back to Clementine, especially in defense of moi. I was, after all, keeping this HUGE SECRET for her.

Clementine must have realized something was off, because she was like, "Katie? You okay?"

Katie blushed. "I—I'm fine," she stammered. "Just worried about getting started on those rewinds we need to work on."

At that point I realized I wasn't going to get anywhere. Mom was already out of the locker room and punching away on her BlackBerry, waiting for me. I gave Clementine my meanest look and stomped away. A fair-and-square vote, she'd said? Yeah, right. Unless by "fair" Clem meant saying no to any idea I came up with. As they say, "All's Fair in Clementine's War." Or maybe that's not the saying, but still, it sounds about right.

On the way home, I was practically boiling. I tried to

GIVE ME A 74!

find a radio station that could match the mood I was feeling. But there weren't any songs about sending a cheerleader to jail for being so mean.

"Hon, you all right?" asked Mom, casting a quick glance in my direction.

I leaned my head against the window and closed my eyes. "Yeah. Sort of. Just annoyed about some school politics stuff."

"Oh," she said. "The fair, you mean?"

"Yeah. Lanie and I had a great idea for a booth and it didn't make it. Which I guess I'd be okay with if I didn't have a feeling the reason we didn't get it had something to do with Clementine."

"I see," she said, chewing her lip. I had a feeling she was trying to come up with something positive and reassuring to say. Because Mom is a true cheerleader through and through. "I'm sure it will all work out." She gave me a quick pat on the shoulder. "And you'll have fun helping with the Dunk the Jock booth," she said brightly.

See?

"Yeah, I guess," I said. "It's more than just that, though." I wanted to say it is more the principle of it than being bummed that I wouldn't get to have a booth with Lanes. Just how unfair it all was.

GIVE ME A 75!

"Well, if it will make you feel any better, I'm making meatball subs tonight," she said.

"Thanks, Mom."

Then an idea came to me. Clementine couldn't be the be-all and end-all. I need to get a real answer and figure this thing out. Tomorrow I'm going to talk to all the other committee members and find out what REALLY happened. Wish me luck!

GIVE ME A
76!

Saturday, April 16

Live! From my breakfast table!

Spirit Level:

Bowl-o-Rama Drama

Oops! Didn't even write about the Grizzlies cheering for Bowling League on Thursday. The team luckily was in better spirits ever since our group huddle, so Jacqui and I got a break from the usual complaints that go along with cheering for the kind of teams that aren't exactly spectator sports.

I also think the Grizzlies can't help but have a bit of sympathy for the members of the Bowling League. They fought SUPER hard to get recognized as a school sport, and it wasn't until just two years ago that they were actually considered one. I can't even count how many bake sales they had before that happened. But as much as I had the rah-rah-rah's for them, I didn't want to admit to the rest of the team that the Bowl-o-Rama used to be a sort of home away from home for me from back in the day when my

GIVE ME A 77!

parents took me there. (we were practically pros!)

The last time I'd been bowling was when Bevan and I went. That seems like FOREVER ago. Luckily, Bevan and I seem cool with one another these days, so it is not awkward when we see each other around school or anything. Phew.

Anyway, when we got to Bowl-o-Rama, there was this cuh-razy fight going on already between the Port Angeles Pin Pals and the Dry Creek Spare Me's. A Port Angeles girl was accusing a Dry Creek girl of purposely dropping a bowling ball on her toe. "It was slippery!" the Dry Creek girl insisted. "I didn't see you standing there."

"You totally saw me standing there, and purposely let it slip from your fingers," said the Port Angeles girl. "Just admit it."

"Oh please," said the Dry Creek girl. "It was a kid-size ball anyway. They're like styrofoam. Get over it."

So the Port Angeles girl spent the rest of the game trying to convince the coaches to disqualify the other girl, but because it happened before the official start of the game, they didn't buy it. Even the Grizzlies look tame compared to those bowling gals. Talk about Bowl-o-Rama drama!

On a cheer-related note, though, the team got almost all the counts right for the Heads Will Roll

GIVE ME A 78!

cheer, and there were only some tiny mistakes in our other cheers. Katarina messed up on a low V, and Ian brought his arm across his body when he should have been in "clean it up" stance. But no one noticed except Jacqui and me. Plus, the league really appreciated that we came up with cheers just for them. Awwwww.

Quick update on the Clementine sitch: On Friday, I luckily ran into Katie by the Lounge before class, and we had a few quick minutes to talk about our plans with Luc (plus some other necessary stuff. More on that soon).

"I'm dying to hear what everyone is up to back in New York," she said. "Like, who got in where, and everything."

I saw Evan walking down the hall talking to one of his friends and smiled in his direction. But not like a "Wow! You just made my day!" kind of dorky smile (wouldn't want to look desperate). Just more of a "Nice. Cool to see ya," kind of smile. He looked a little surprised at seeing Katie and me together, gave me a quick salute, and disappeared around the corner.

"So I just really hope Luc gives us the inside scoop on all those girls," Katie continued. I'd zoned out during my Evan spotting, so I hope I didn't miss anything important. Oops! Space-cadet Madison.

GIVE ME A 79!

"I'm sure Luc will fill you in on everything under the sun," I said.

She looked down at her mega adorbs white ballet flats with little cherries on them (must find similar pair ASAP) and sighed. "Yeah. I just feel like sometimes those girls have the perfect lives. Like nothing ever goes wrong."

I was like "'Scuse me? Katie Parker feels like her life is less than perfect?" (Jaw on floor.) It is kind of funny because I always think of Katie as having everything in her life go perfectly. Like, how could you not be on top of the world when you're beautiful, popular, and the captain of the varsity cheerleading team?

The sane part of my brain knows that no one has the perfect life, and especially now that I've gotten to know her, I realize she has problems like the rest of us. But the other part of me can't help but look at her and think how lucky she is. It's kind of nice to know that even Katie Parker has Katie Parkers in her life.

I half expected her to mention something about what happened the other night after practice between Clementine and me, but she said nothing. Not that I'm surprised. I couldn't help myself, though—I just had to speak up.

GIVE ME AN 80!

"Okay, so don't get mad," I said, giving her a little heads-up. I squished in closer to where she was standing so no one would hear us talk. "But is it just me or is Clementine acting even meaner than usual?"

"Meaner, like, how?" asked Katie.

"I mean, she seems to be really unreasonable about Lanie's and my booth idea. You don't really think there was a 'vote,' do you?"

Katie's eyes flickered with uncertainty for a moment, so I knew she must have seen at least a little of what I was talking about even if she wouldn't admit it. "Well, I don't know. I think whatever is happening with Clem is more complicated than you think. She's been under a lot of pressure from her mom lately."

This was a surprise. Clem, with a problem? Guess I'm always overestimating people and their so-called perfect lives. "Her mom?"

"Yeah," said Katie in an almost-whisper. "It was her mom's idea to do the styling advice booth for the Titans. Of course, Clementine told the team it was her idea. And I didn't have a problem with it. But anyway, her mom wants to 'reach a younger demographic' and thought that making a celebrity appearance at the fair would be her ticket."

"Oh," was all I could say. I found it hard to process

GIVE ME AN 8!!

the image of someone—even her own mom—forcing
Clementine into doing anything. I've never seen that girl
not get her way. I can't even imagine what she must
have been like as a toddler.

"I know it's hard to understand. But I think Clem
doesn't mean half the obnoxious things she says. A lot
of it has to do with her own bad stuff going on. Maybe
try to talk to her when she's not at practice, or not
with me?"

I was going to say that I'd tried that, sort of, in
the hallways, but each time she'd ignored me. I guess
I wasn't going to get much sympathy from Katie.
Maybe if I try talking to Clementine one on one again
on Monday, I'll have some more luck. We'll see . . . but I
don't have a good feeling about this.

GIVE ME AN
82!

DERP

Monday, April 18
Après lunch, outside the caf
Spirit Level:
Getting to the Bottom of the
Mystery Pyramid

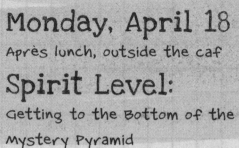

I guess most of the day has been pretty good. Evan tapped me on the shoulder when I was stuffing a quick PB&J down my throat. No time for a leisurely lunch when there are Fair Committee members to harass! He was wearing one of my favorite Evan looks: a too-small button-down shirt (frayed at the elbows), a light scarf (he'd gotten into scarves lately, but it looked kind of cool on him), and slightly-too-short jeans. Now I know that short jeans can look like your family exclusively shops at the Salvation Army, but on Evan it looked almost . . . trendy. I still don't know how the clothes that I considered Major Dorkville on him before now look so cute to me.

"What's up, sticky fingers?" he said, nodding toward my sandwich. "Haven't spoken to you all weekend."

He was right, though. I'd been so wrapped up in the

GIVE ME A
83!

fair drama and working on Get Up and Cheer! stuff
that I didn't have any Evan time at all. Which is weird,
since he is usually on my mind most of the day. I am
TOO STRESSED!

"Yeah, I've been busy with cheer stuff and this
whole booth drama with Clementine."

"That's cool," he said. "I just missed talking to you
this weekend, is all." I saw him flush slightly.

"Well, you could have called me," I said jokingly. "The
phone works both ways."

Evan smiled. "I know you're a busy girl. I didn't want
to bother you, with your **CRAZY** schedule and all."
He waved his hands in the air to emphasize the word
"crazy."

"Nice save," I said.

But I really wanted to spend more time with Evan,
even though I had a lot going on. So I had an idea:

"Do you, um, need any help getting your booth
together for next week?" I asked.

Evan's eyes seemed to sparkle at the suggestion.
"Definitely. I need to pick the 'best of' from SuperBoy
and mount those images on foam core, so people can
choose which scene they'd want me to replicate but
with them drawn in the picture. Like a personalized
SuperBoy sketch."

GIVE ME AN
84!

"I can do that."

"You free later today?" he asked.

I nodded.

"Awesome. All right, some of us gotta get a real lunch," he said, cuing his exit.

"Enjoy your chow," I said. "See you later."

Seriously, even the idea of just hanging out in Evan's grungy old room with a bunch of foam core and glue makes me feel giddy!

The next order of business (the not fun order) was locating the different committee members to ask them what the real deal was about me and Lanie not getting a booth. Lanie had been so miserable last night when I talked to her about it, because already she was getting hounded by the Fair Committee to sign up for trash pickup. And even though Lanie's a good sport, she's not really into physical labor. I can't imagine anyone being that excited about picking up sticky Popsicle wrappers and cotton candy cones while everyone else is enjoying rides and hanging out at booths. She'd tried to talk to Clementine too, but with the same results as me: Clem claimed her stupid "you were outvoted" thing again and that was the end of discussion. I'd already talked to Jared about it, and he'd said the only person who didn't want two fashion-themed booths was Clementine

GIVE ME AN 85!

herself. And there wasn't a vote at all, she just declared that it wouldn't make sense to have both and crossed ours out.

"Why didn't you say something?" I'd asked Jared. He'd literally cowered at the suggestion.

"Honestly? That girl scares me. Most people didn't want to say anything she'd disagree with."

"Yeah, yeah. I get your point."

LAME-O.

But I needed more than just Jared's word as ammunition. My plan was to ask enough people around the cafeteria so that when I went to Principal Gershon, there'd be evidence to back up what I was saying (and hopefully people would speak honestly about it if she asked them). I caught another Kiss-Up Crew (er, Fair Committee) member—Helen Bassett—on her way into the cafeteria. When I asked her why we didn't get the booth we wanted, she apologized.

"I'm really sorry. Clementine was in a real mood about it. I tried to defend your idea, because I thought it was really cute, but she was super mean about it and really chewed my head off when I tried."

I could see why Helen didn't want to rock the boat with Clem, ever since the Nose-Picking Incident of last year, when Clementine caught Helen itching her nostril.

GIVE ME AN 86!

Of course Clem took that opportunity to claim that Helen was a giant nose picker, and Helen couldn't enter a room without someone asking her, "Find anything good?"

Tracey Mesnick was easy to find too. All I had to do was look for the nearest crowd of girls and there was Tracey in the middle. I wasn't the least bit surprised that she'd also joined Kiss-Up Crew too. She's Port Angeles's answer to Gossip Girl, and if anyone would want to know and help be in charge of who is doing what at the school fair, it would be her. When I finally tore Tracey from her audience, she too said that no one had a problem with our booth except Clementine. But because Clem had veto power, her word was the last one.

"Yeah, there was no denying that girl what she wanted," said Tracey. "And she did NOT want your booth in the picture, for some reason." I could practically see the wheels turning in Tracey's head as she tried to figure out why Clementine has a beef with me. Before I could walk away, she asked the million-dollar question: "Speaking of, why do you think she didn't want you to have that booth?"

"No idea." I shrugged innocently. I had to get out of there before she attempted to read my mind or

GIVE ME AN 87!

something. "Thanks, Tracey."

This is great (not). So I can pretty much guarantee that by tomorrow, the school paper will have a full report on the Clementine Prescott vs. Madison Hays issue.

I quickly texted Lanie what my cafeteria sleuthing had turned up so far, and she wrote, "That's it. We r taking this on with Principal G."

But I told her I wanted to try approaching Clementine one more time before we became tattletale types running to the principal for help.

"Well, if u put it that wayyyy, I guess . . . fine."

I told Lanie to meet me at the caf, and we'd go up to Clementine together. "But move it! We don't have that long."

Lanie rushed over in a nanosecond and apologized but then got right down to business. "So where is our favorite person? At her usual table?"

"Yeah. I saw her lording over there when I went to grab a sandwich," I said, nodding my head in the direction of the table where Clem was seated.

It was the usual Titan Triumvirate: Katie was sitting between Clementine and Hilary, while a bunch of guys drooled over the three of them.

It was too bad Clementine wasn't alone, because with

GIVE ME A 88!

an audience, I knew she'd lay the mean on superthick. But this was going to be my last try at talking some sense into her, and I doubted I'd find her alone practically ever.

"You sure you want to do this?" asked Lanie.

I knew what she meant. Neither of us was "scared" to talk to Clementine, but who knew what kind of scene she'd cause in front of all the football guys and the rest of the cafeteria? I could just see the withering look she'd give me before she hurled one of her famous one-liners my way. There I would stand, tongue-tied and humiliated as their entire table (but hopefully not Katie) laughed at me.

Quick trip down memory lane: About a year or so ago, there was this one time Clem decided not to invite her teammate Marissa Kemper to a party at her house that the entire rest of the team had been invited to. Clem had been ignoring Marissa for days, and finally Marissa worked up the courage to say something about it. Everyone who had been in the gym at the time could hear Clem's stinging words:

"I'm sorry. Did someone just say something?"

Marissa had held her ground. "Yeah, I did."

"Oh right, yes, you did," Clementine had said. "Except I don't really waste my breath on loser

GIVE ME AN
89!

cheerleaders who can't even stay on top of a simple pyramid. Cheerleaders who almost cost us our shot at Regionals."

It was true—Marissa had taken a heck of a fall at the Regional Qualifier, and the Titans had almost lost out on going to Regionals because of it. Girlfriend paid a price, though: she had to go on crutches for weeks and watch the Titans from the sidelines. Which is basically a cheerleader's worst nightmare. No one likes to be left out of competing in something they've worked their butts off to participate in. It is kind of like seeing a whole tray of desserts in front of you and not being able to reach out and grab one because your hands are shackled to a wall.

Marissa had stood there, her fists clenched at her sides and her eyes welling up with tears. "It wasn't my fault! It was an ACCIDENT!"

"Whatevs. This party is for Titans who've got game. The only ACCIDENT I saw was your TRAIN WRECK of a routine."

News of the fight spread around the school faster than a cold virus. Before she knew it, even non-Titans were teasing Marissa. Wherever she went, someone would mumble, "Train wreck."

Marissa had almost quit after that, but finally

GIVE ME A 90!

Coach Whipley had said something to Clem about being less of a bully and made her apologize. Of course, I have a feeling Coach Whipley just said that because she wanted to keep World's Worst Bully as her own personal title.

Anyway, breaking down in the cafeteria and earning a fancy new nickname was NOT on my list of things to do today, so I made up my mind that no matter what Clem said, I'd stay strong. Besides, I had Lanie by my side. Best Friend Power!

We walked up to the Titan table. Clem was laughing at something one of the guys had just said. "Ohmigod, John, shut UP!" she squealed. Whenever she flirts, her voice seems to rise ten levels higher. "You're gonna make me spit up my iced tea!"

Lanie cleared her throat loudly to try to get Clem's attention. "Excuse me, sorry to interrupt," said Lanie, who clearly wasn't.

Clementine casually sipped her drink and sighed, addressing her crowd of admirers. "Calm down, everyone. Don't be alarmed. I'm sure these two are just lost. Sorry, ladies," she said, turning to face us. "But Dorkville is thataway." She pointed to the table where Evan, Lanes, and I usually sat.

"Don't worry. We're not staying," I said. "Listen, we

GIVE ME A 911!

spoke to everyone on the Fair Committee, and it looks like there **WAS** no vote. You were the **ONLY** one who didn't want our booth to make it."

How I was able to say all this in one breath without stuttering or getting beet red is a mystery I may never solve.

"Hmm, so strange," said Clementine, tapping her mouth with her forefinger. "I could have sworn we all voted against it." She grabbed a carrot stick off Hilary's plate and took a dainty bite. "Oh well. Too late now!"

"Actually, it's not too late," said Lanie. "We're taking this to Principal G if you don't straighten this out."

Clem coughed at the mention of getting the principal involved. I knew this would hit her right where we wanted. The last thing Clem wanted was to look bad in the school's eyes. Otherwise, how would she be able to sweet-talk them into doing special things for the Titans that other teams don't get?

"Excuse me?" she asked.

"You heard us," I said. "Principal G said that if something can't be figured out with you or the Fair Committee, then a student could go to her. And since I have each Fair Committee member saying that there never was a unanimous vote against our booth, I think we

GIVE ME A 92!

have every reason in the world to go over your head."

Katie, who'd already pushed her food away so she could watch this little scene, gave Clem a meaningful look. "Clementine . . . ."

Clem scowled at her plate. "Fine," she said.

"Fine?" asked Lanie. "Fine what?"

"Do your stupid booth. What do I care? Just don't blame me when everyone flocks to the Titans' booth for fashion advice instead of yours."

"That's a risk we're willing to take," I said. "A LOW risk," I added for good measure. I gave Lanie a tiny nudge, letting her know this was our cue to walk away.

"Yeah, have fun with that," said Clem, always trying to have the last word.

When we were finally out of earshot of the Titan table, Lanie gave me a high five. "We did it! We have our booth back!"

I definitely was happy about what we had just accomplished, but I had a feeling there'd be a hefty price to pay for having threatened one of the Queen Bees. Clementine does not like losing her battles, so even though we "won" this time, I knew she'd have something else up her sleeve within minutes. Oh well. At least Lanie isn't going to be stuck doing trash pickup at the fair anymore. V for victory, right?

GIVE ME A 93!

Ugh, not looking forward to Grizzly practice later. I know, I know. Totally uncaptainlike.

BEFORE SNOOZEVILLE, ABOUT TO HAVE SWEET DREAMS (I HOPE!)

Yep, I was right. Grizzly practice was pretty harsh. Our Beyoncé-inspired moves are not going as well as Jacqui and I had hoped.

Throughout practice, Ian and Matt keep asking to do more break-dance-type moves instead of what they call "girl power moves." I think they're lucky we're doing a military-style dance instead of one of the more girl-type dances we could have come up with. They don't see it that way, unforch. **ALSO**, Katarina's new thing is to start, like, everything a second too early. Like, I'll say "Five, six, seven, eight," and she'll be doing her low V at "four." Frustration Nation!!!

Evan and I grabbed some slices to go after practice, and this time when he ordered he told the cashier that it was just one order. Meaning, he paid for me before I could even throw my bills on the counter. So at this point I was like, Mystery Time: Was that a "date move" or a "really nice friend" move? Like, back in the day, when we were just best buds, he never would have paid for me. In fact, if we were in, say, the candy store, he used

GIVE ME A 94!

to always weasel an extra pack of gum in there, and when I'd turn to ask him to pay up, he'd laugh and duck out the door (super sneaky). Lanie is so lucky that she knows that Marc likes her. It must make things much easier. Not that they go out on pizza dates that often, but I'm sure if they had to download some dusty old archive or something together, he'd offer to do it for both of them. And she wouldn't have to guess what it meant because SHE'D ALREADY KNOW.

So after pizza, we went back to his house and chatted about the usual stuff. His dad asked us if we wanted to watch a TV special about some old baseball player who neither of us really cares about, but Evan said we had work to do. We sat in his room with just the light from his desk lamp on, which gave it a cozy, romantic feel (at least for me). He grabbed a stack of papers and plopped them on my lap.

"So here are the ones I'm choosing from for the fair. What do you think? Do they scream 'SuperBoy: Best Of' to you?"

I considered each one carefully, and every now and then I'd look up at Evan to catch him looking at me kind of weird.

"Didn't you have a sketch where SuperBoy has this long cape on and is drinking a slushie? I always thought

GIVE ME A 95!

that was cute. And for people who want their own drawing, you can take that scene and personalize it by drawing that person in the scene. Maybe that person will be begging SuperBoy to help him save the day or something?"

He started digging through his piles of papers, looking for that particular scene. "I like it! Good thinking, Madison."

"That's what I'm here for. I'm the thinker."

We figured out a top-ten list of best SuperBoy images, and then worked on making signs for his booth. I knew I should probs also be working with Lanie on our booth now that we had it approved (finally), but working on SuperBoy was an excuse to hang with Evan. While we were making signs, he kept nudging me playfully with the end of his marker, so I took my marker and drew on him (which of course made him want to retaliate).

"That's it! You asked for it!" he said, coming at me with the tip of a sharpie.

Next thing I knew, he was trying to pin my arm down to the floor. And even though I'm the athletic one of the two of us, I couldn't break free. Finally, my wrist was on the floor, and we were both laughing hysterically.

"I surrender!" I said between giggles.

GIVE ME A 96!

He started drawing on my arm (which gave me major goose bumps), and when he was finished, I had a sort of cool-looking cheerleader superhero on my arm.

"Thanks, E, I'll never wash it off," I joked, batting my eyelashes.

"You shouldn't. It will be worth millions someday."

"Yeah, I don't know if I can hold off a shower THAT long."

Before it was time for me to head home, Evan did something I never thought he'd do. Or, at least, hadn't expected him to do after all this weirdness between us. He ASKED ME OUT ON A DATE. (Thank goodness he didn't do that with indelible ink on my arm. That would have been kinda embarrassing.) He didn't say it like, "Let's go on a date." It was more like, "Can I take you out somewhere on Friday?" I almost did a herkie right then and there. Talk about embarrassing! And it was totally different from the time he asked me to Just Desserts, because back then he had just said he wanted me to "check it out" with him. But he said the words "take you out," so I am pretty almost 100% sure this couldn't be confused with "not a date." Right?

"Um, yeah," I said, trying not to sound too excited. "Where?"

GIVE ME A 97!

"Leave that to me," he said, like he'd been planning dates his whole life. "I'll pick you up at seven, and I'll see if someone can drive us."

"Cool," I said, my head spinning.

I walked home on cloud nine. Or maybe in this case it is cloud ten, because nine just seems so average. Isn't everyone ELSE floating there?

I speed-dialed Lanes to tell her the BIG NEWS.

"Whassup?" said Lanie.

"OMG," I said. "You are going to fall out of your chair when I tell you this."

"Yeeeessss?" she said.

"Evan asked me out on a date!" I said.

"Yeah, FINALLY!" said Lanes. "Wait, are you sure, Mads?" Count on Lanie to be the party pooper. Or cloud popper, or whatever.

"Well, he said the words 'take you out,' so I think so," I said, trying not to let doubt creep into my brain.

"He actually said those words? Not like, 'Let's go to this place' on Friday?"

I did a little rewind of the whole scene in my head, just to make sure I hadn't hallucinated the whole thing.

"Yes, Lanie. Yes, I'm positive that that is what he said. I mean, I guess I can't be entirely sure, but it SOUNDS to me like a date. Right?"

GIVE ME A 98!

"I'd have to say yeah. That **DOES** sound like a date. Go, little E."

I don't know why it annoys me just a little that she still calls him that, since to me he's no longer "little E," the boy who used to star as the husband in all our playing-house episodes. Now he's "completely adorable and crush-worthy Evan," to me at least. But I guess I can see it being hard for Lanie to picture him that way, even now. I mean, it was hard for ME, too, at first.

Okay, must catch some z's. I'm so definitely going to be dreaming about this date. Now, what in the world am I going to wear???

GIVE ME A 99!

Friday, April 22

Five seconds before class

Spirit Level:

Afternoon ~~Delight~~ Disaster

I woke up this morning going completely nuts thinking about my date later that night with the E-Man. It just felt so surreal, imagining him coming to my doorstep to pick me up. I tried to picture what it would be like, but my brain wouldn't process it. Would he be holding flowers? Would he be nervous? Would he like what I was wearing? Speaking of, here is what I decided on: skinny jeans with a long flowy silky top, long dangly earrings, and the platforms I had to beg Mom to let me buy. Footnote: Mom was worried I'd break my neck in them, but I pointed out that with me being a cheerleader, there are far worse ways for me to injure myself. That seemed to do the trick ☺. But anyway, I think the outfit says "cute" without trying too hard. Like if I wore a dress, that could be too much, and I obvs wasn't going to wear sneakers and any old shirt.

GIVE ME A 100!

I think the silk of the top and the earrings take everything up a notch. Hope Evan agrees!

On my way to school I was in happy la-la land, listening to a Bruno Mars song on the radio and probably smiling like an idiot. Mom kept giving me funny looks. Like, what? She's never seen me happy before? Please. Okay, fine, maybe SOMETIMES I get a little moody. I didn't tell her about my date with Evan, because I didn't want her to get all gushy and teary-eyed. I could totally see her doing the "Wow, my little girl is growing up so fast" look. Or she would treat Evan weirdly. Yeah, no thanks.

But right after lunch, disaster struck. Of course Madison Hays is not allowed to have one drama-free day. No sirree. My phone buzzed with an SOS text from Lanes.

"Srsly, call me," it read.

I ducked into a corner and rang her up. "Where are you?" she asked, without even saying hello.

"Just leaving the caf. Where were you at lunch?" Evan hadn't been at lunch either that day, because he had some extra-credit thing he was doing, and I didn't exactly appreciate eating alone at our table. But it happens.

"I'm really sorry, but that's what I'm calling about,"

GIVE ME A
101!

said Lanie, sounding miserable. "I popped into the <u>Daily</u> <u>Angeles</u> to drop an article off before lunch and to say hi to Marc."

"Yeah, why am I not surprised?" I said.

"No, that's not the story! So I was there, and Marc was there, and then there's this knock on the door."

"Just hold on a sec. Are you anywhere near the caf?"

"Yeah."

"Let's meet on the steps, okay?"

Lanie didn't bother responding before she cut off our call.

I met her on the steps and realized something bad must have happened, because her forehead was all crinkled with worry, and her eyeliner looked like she'd done it in the dark.

"Lanes, you might want to look in a mirror," I said.

She scowled. "Ugh, I was doing my usual afternoon reapplication but must have been so upset I wasn't paying attention. Thanks for catching that, Mads."

"Okay, so dish."

Lanie explained that the knock on the door was Miss Clementine Prescott herself. Lanie had no idea why Clem had decided to grace the <u>Daily Angeles</u> with her presence, but she'd immediately gotten the feeling that Clem was up to no good. Clem barely looked at Lanes

GIVE ME A 102!

and walked right up to Marc, who hadn't even noticed her come in.

"Ahem," Clementine had said, even though Lanie was already looking at her. But it was Marc's attention she wanted.

"Yeah?" Lanie had said.

"I'm here to talk to Marc. Marc, I have an awesome idea for one of your stories about the fair."

Marc had finally looked up from the piece he was reading and nodded at her to speak.

"Since I'm the Head Fair Leader, I pretty much have the inside scoop on everything fair related. So I was thinking, wouldn't it be fabulous if the paper did an intimate profile on my involvement with the fair, and how I'm single-handedly making the whole thing come together?"

Marc had just looked at her like she'd landed from Planet Cheerleader.

Clementine hadn't missed a beat. She twirled a finger through her hair and sat down right next to Marc. "I think it would be the perfect way to show how a student can have more than one interest and talent. I'm a born leader, obviously, but you wouldn't expect a cheerleader to also be so involved in the community, right?"

At this point, Lanie said, Clementine couldn't have

GIVE ME A
103!

been batting her eyelashes more furiously. Lanie couldn't take it anymore.

"Bossing people around for the school fair isn't exactly the work of Mother Teresa," she countered.

Clem had just continued smiling like an idiot at Marc, as if Lanie wasn't even in the room. "Thanks for your input, Lanie, but this is between Marc and me. I want a more SERIOUS staff writer to do my profile."

Finally Marc had snapped out of his "what is this girl talking about" face and spoke up. "I appreciate the compliment, but we'd definitely need to take this up with the rest of the staff to make sure it's a piece that everyone agrees on."

Lanie had been so happy that Marc had come up with a good excuse. And also that he wasn't buying into her obvious attempts at flirtation.

Clementine had finally gotten up from the table then. "No biggie. I just thought I'd give you the idea. At no charge, of course!" she'd said with a flirtatious giggle.

"Madison!" said Lanie, pulling nervously at the bottom strands of her hair. "She was hitting on Marc! She's trying to steal him away so she can work her weird cheerleader voodoo magic on him."

GIVE ME A 104!

"Lanie, you have nothing to worry about with Marc. Didn't you just say he was the one who came up with the excuse to turn her down? And how he hardly noticed her when she walked into the room in the first place?"

"Yeah, I guess," Lanie agreed softly. "But the point is, Clementine is trying to get in between Marc and me. And I don't think it has anything to do with her liking him or anything. I think she just wants to punish me—or us—for getting our booth back."

I'm not trying to be super egotistical or anything, thinking that the entire world revolves around me, but I can't help but think that Clem was trying to teach ME a lesson by hurting my best friend. Cuz normally she doesn't have anything against Lanie (except her association with me), and until now, it's really just been me who Clem has been mega obnoxious toward. Me, me, me, me, meeee (how many times can I write that word on a page?)! And now I feel really bad that Lanie is getting the Torture Treatment from Clem, probably because of me. I knew that giving us the booth wouldn't come without complications.

"Don't worry," I told Lanie. "You've obviously got nothing to worry about with Marc and Clementine. I'll see if maybe I can talk to Katie about it and see what

GIVE ME A 105!

she says. Maybe she can talk to Clementine about backing off a little."

Lanie nodded, but that furrow in her brow was still there. I texted Katie in front of Lanie to tell her to meet me in our room ASAP. Luckily, we both had a free period after lunch. I needed to get through to Katie that this stuff with Clementine was getting kind of ridiculous. And since Clem would practically jump off a cliff to avoid talking to me, and because she was Katie's BFF, I figured I had a better shot of having Katie get through to her.

I got to the room a few minutes before Katie and collected my thoughts. I thought about the things that had been happening lately with Clementine and tried to make some sense of them. First, I guess around the time I decided not to join the Titans was when she started just generally being meaner to me than usual. Then she tried to sabotage my booth with Lanie. THEN she tried to get in between Lanie and her boy. If it were just one solitary thing, I wouldn't really think much of it. (They don't call Clementine a Queen Bee for nothing. Being mean is part of the package.) But now that these other things are piling up, I can't help but think there's more to this. BUT WHAT IS IT???

Katie came bouncing into the room, ponytail

GIVE ME A 106!

swinging, with her usual face full of sunshine and her perfect cheerleader smile. But as soon as she saw the expression on my face, she must have known something was up.

"What's going on? Did something happen?" she asked.

I explained the latest in the Clementine vs. Madison saga. Katie chewed on her lip thoughtfully.

"Wow," she said. "I guess Clem is kind of acting strange."

"Yeah, you think?"

Katie sat on top of the desk next to mine and rhythmically drummed her pink fingernails against the wood. "I just don't understand what's gotten into her. I know she's having a hard time with her mom and the booth and everything, but I don't know why she's taking it all out on you."

"I have no idea, except maybe she's super mad that I didn't join the Titans. But I was thinking . . ." I paused because I didn't want to sound like a loser when I said what I was about to say. "Maybe you want to tell her that you're my friend, and that the way she's acting is not cool?"

Basically the way I see it is that if Clementine knew that Katie and I were friends, and if Katie made a request AS MY FRIEND for Clem to change her

GIVE ME A
107!

'tude toward me, then maybe Clem would listen. I mean, Katie and I have been going to great lengths to act like strangers whenever Clem sees us near each other. She probably thinks that during the times we do talk, we're just comparing cheer captain notes or something. Which up until lately was pretty fine with me. But now that I'm keeping secrets from Evan (can't tell him about Luc) and Clem has gone a little overboard, I think it is time Katie tells her what's what. Don't friends defend one another?

Unfortunately, Katie didn't see it my way. "Madison, I can't do that. I can't tell her about our friendship. Not without explaining my trip to New York."

I wish I could have come up with a loophole in her reasoning—some way for her to avoid dishing the details about New York while explaining how we got to be friends. But the whole reason the two of us became un-frenemied was because of our bonding in New York. We'd have to come up with some elaborate lie otherwise, and honestly I don't have room in my brain for that kind of thing.

"I can't tell Clementine about the audition," she continued. "It would be a disaster. I even tried the other day, but something held me back. I feel so bad about lying, but now it's gone on so long she'll be so mad

GIVE ME A 108!

when I tell her the truth. I feel like Clem will flip out about me even thinking about leaving the Titans. Please, please don't say anything to her."

Katie was getting a little hysterical. Wow, this really was a day for friend drama.

"Okay, okay," I said, my hands up in surrender. "I'm not gonna say anything, don't worry."

"I know it's hard to understand, but Clem and I have been best friends practically forever. Like you and Lanie. And Clem has been a good friend, even if it is just me she's good to."

I wanted to say there were a couple of BIG differences here . . . but I just kept my mouth shut. I didn't want Katie to have some kind of major meltdown. Maybe if I bring it up another time, I'll have more luck. In the meantime, though, I'm definitely on my own with this.

Later on, before cheer practice, Lanes and I met up outside the gym. I told her about my conversation FAIL with Katie.

"Some friend SHE is," said Lanie, shaking her head. "I told you not to trust cheerleaders."

"Um, excuse me?" I said, raising an eyebrow.

"Fine, maybe just Titan cheerleaders. Seriously, what is her deal? Aren't you tired of this whole 'secret friendship' of yours?"

GIVE ME A
109!

"Yeah, I am. But what am I going to do?"

Lanie shook her head in frustration. "Whatever. The good thing is, Marc said he'd sooner stick a pencil in his eye than spend time interviewing Clementine. Luckily, he has an aversion to anything pink and peppy."

"Nice," I said. "In other news, though, tonight's my date with Evan." I quickly scanned the hall to make sure Evan wasn't sitting there. Lately, I never really know when he'll pop up, which makes talking about him a tiny bit difficult.

Lanie's face lit up. "You psyched?"

I nodded. "Psyched and a little nervous."

Lanie gave me some pointers, because now that she and Marc are kind of together, she considers herself the dating expert. I mean, yeah, I did go out with Bevan a few times, but since that didn't work out, I guess Lanie wins this one.

"Okay, well, here are some of the things I've learned. Ahem." She crossed her arms in a very ladylike way, and then gave me her ultimate dating do's and don'ts list.

(And now I'll just sum up the best ones of the bunch here in a LIST, because I heart lists):

GIVE ME A 110!

LANIE'S LIST OF DATING DO'S AND DON'TS

Don't laugh too hard. Especially when eating. We
    don't want food coming out of one's nose.

Try to anticipate gentlemanly gestures, i.e., the
    pulling out of a chair. Otherwise you're bound to
    bump into each other when you both go to reach
    for it, and that would be awkward.

If you think something unseemly might be stuck on
    your face (think food, or a booger) don't try to
    wipe it away. You'll just draw more attention to
    it. Just calmly excuse yourself and go to the
    ladies' room. Or unisex bathroom, if that is the
    situation.

    It still is hilarious to me that I have to follow ANY
type of rules with Evan. But I'm glad Lanie is being
supportive about all this. It must be even weirder
for her that her two friends are going out. Gaaaah!
Nervous!

LATER, POST THE GREAT DATE

    Sittin' up in my room, going over the details of the
night. Thank goodness I had practice earlier, because

GIVE ME A
!!!!

it got rid of all that adrenaline I'd been storing up.
I completely rocked our dance routine for Get Up
and Cheer! And everyone could tell I was into it, so
it pumped up the rest of the team too. Even Ian and
Matt were woohooing at the end of practice, because
of all the good vibes going around. Mom kept looking
at us with a dorky proud parent smile. I know she has
high hopes for us for this competition. We better not
mess up!

I asked Mom if we could hustle home after
practice. Thankfully, she agreed to skip one of her
nightly errands and said she'd stop in at the pharmacy
another time. Yay! So I had more time to primp and
mentally prepare myself for my date. I tried to take
the same approach to getting ready for this date as
I do with getting ready for a cheer competition. First
I told myself positive things like, "Everything will be
cool, and you will NOT accidentally drop brown-colored
food onto Evan's lap this time." Then I sat on my bed
and channeled a "winning attitude," which is similar to
praying to Ye Olde Cheer Gods, but instead of picturing
my usual pom-pom-wearing gods, I tried to conjure up
the kind of gods that might help in a dating situation.
Which, I don't know, means maybe they're wearing fancy
outfits and holding boxes of chocolates? Hmm.

GIVE ME A
112!

Finally, it was time to primp. Tonight would require a lot less makeup than a cheer competition, but probably the same amount of thought behind it. I wanted a look that said "effort" but not "trying too hard." So I grabbed a lip gloss that was just a shade darker than what I usually wear, put some mascara on, and swept on the expensive blush that I save only for special occasions. Then I did a cute little messy side braid the way I've been seeing them do in the teen magazines and fastened a glittery hair clip. Voilà!

Of course my favorite part of getting ready was putting on my outfit. I was glad I'd decided what to wear in advance, otherwise I could have spent hours changing my mind. Just as I was spritzing a vanilla body spray, Mom called up from downstairs.

"Madison!" she yelled. "Evan's down here!"

I could hear that her voice wasn't in the range of her usual octave—which meant that she could tell something was going on. Usually when Evan comes over, she'll just yell gruffly, "Madison! Evan!" but today I could hear just a little bit of a different tone. Like, "Ooh, Madison has a DATE!" I hope she doesn't grill me later about this.

When I got to the landing of the stairs, it was, like, totally out of a movie. Evan was standing down

GIVE ME A 113!

there with his hands in his pockets, looking up at me awkwardly. I could feel his eyes on me as I took each step. My heart was going a million miles a minute I was so nervous. Luckily, Mom had exited the premises for this "lovely" little moment between E and me.

"You look r-really pretty," Evan stammered.

"Thank you," I said, trying not to blush. "You look nice too."

He'd definitely taken some time to get ready too. His hair actually stood in one direction instead of all over the place—but Evan being Evan, it looked like he might have overdone it in the hair gel department.

And even though I think his vintage wardrobe (okay, technically it's hand-me-downs) is cute, I liked that he was wearing a newish-looking button-down shirt and jeans that covered his ankles.

"You ready?" he asked.

I grabbed my bag and called good-bye to Mom. "Yep."

We walked toward the direction of Main Street, making silly small talk like two strangers meeting for the first time, as if we never hung out for hours just surfing the Internet or watching horror-movie marathons.

"So where are we going?"

Evan rubbed his hands together nervously. "La Dolce

GIVE ME A 114!

Vita sound good?" he said, like he was hoping I'd approve.

"Oh, I love that place!" La Dolce Vita was the number one date spot for the kids at school in our hood. It wasn't fancy-schmancy (read: Beth would never go there), but it wasn't like a regular pizza place. For example, all pizzas and pastas were served on REAL plates, not paper, and the tables had nice tablecloths instead of that vinyl-checked stuff that for some reason always feels sticky.

When we got to the restaurant, Evan tried to hold the door open for me, but the handle slipped out of his hands at the last second, and the door slammed into my face.

"Ow!" I said, cradling my nose.

Evan looked horrified. "I am SO sorry," he said, reaching to touch my nose. I ducked away instinctively. "It's all right," I assured him, even though I worried that something might have broken.

When the birds stopped flying around my head, the waitress led us to a cozy-looking booth that was so small we had no choice but to sit next to each other, French-style.

I could tell Evan was trying hard not to bump my knee. Before the awkward pause in our convo got even worse, the waitress came by and wordlessly plopped

GIVE ME A 115!

some waters and menu on the table.

"Again, I'm sorry," said Evan, looking at me worriedly.

I smiled reassuringly. "Don't worry about it," I said.

I did a quick scan of the place to make sure no one we knew from school was there. I wasn't embarrassed or anything to be with Evan (quite the opposite!), but the last thing I needed was for our date to become front-page news in the Daily Angeles. No thanks.

"So, what are you in the mood for?" he asked me.

I quickly looked over the menu, but I was pretty sure I wouldn't change my mind from my usual favorite Italian dish: pasta alla Norma. It's rigatoni with eggplant and ricotta. Yumminess! I briefly considered linguini with clam sauce but could just see myself grinning unsuspectingly back at Evan with olive oil dripping down my chin. (That would be in violation of Lanie's Rule #3.) Uh, not hot.

"I think I'll go with pasta alla Norma," I said.

When the waitress came by and asked what we wanted, Evan blurted out, "She'll have," at the same time that I said, "I'll have," because I didn't realize he was planning on ORDERING for me. Old-fashioned much? We finally got through ordering, though, without any further mishaps. And at that point, I was pretty sure we were on a date.

GIVE ME A 116!

Thank goodness we were able to move into our usual comfortable conversation by the time the bread basket arrived. I was too nervous to eat my usual "first course" of bread and oil, which I guess wasn't a bad thing, because the pasta was DE-LISH.

"So what are you up to this weekend?" he asked between mouthfuls of spaghetti and meatballs.

I was about to tell him about Katie's and my plans with Luc, but stopped when I remembered that like everything having to do with Katie, this was something on the DL.

"Just doing cheer stuff, and heading to sew what? for some booth supplies," I lied. I immediately felt horrible as soon as I said it. Lying to Evan was not on my list of favorite things to do. "What about you?" I asked, trying to change the subject.

"Nothing too exciting," he said. "I'm helping my family with some spring cleaning. Maybe I'll hang out with my cousin. Dunno." He shrugged. "If you were free, we could hang out."

I knew I was supposed to work with Lanes on booth stuff Sunday and catch up on a ton of homework. Saturday was out of the question. "Ugh, this weekend really stinks for plans."

I could see his face fall a little. "No worries," he said. When dessert came, he did something INCREDIBLE.

GIVE ME A 117!

He reached across the table. "This is pretty," he said, pointing to the sparkly bangle I was wearing.

"Thanks." I rotated my wrist so he could see the rest of it.

He ran his finger along its edges, and I flinched when he grazed my skin. Then he wrapped his hand around mine. I felt like I was burning a fever, like, a hundred and ten degrees, and wondered if he could tell.

"Is . . . is this okay?" he asked.

I nodded, but inside I was like, "OMG! OMG!" I couldn't wait to tell Lanie about it and thought that this was waaaay better than holding hands while doing research (Lanie and Marc style). But Lanie may not agree.

The waitress came by and wordlessly dropped off the bill, which Evan swept up before I could do anything about it.

"Hey," I said. "Let's split it. Neither of us is rolling in dough."

He shook his head. "Speak for yourself. I've been selling SuperBoys like hotcakes. We're good."

"Well, um, thanks," I said, reeling from what all this meant. Evan and I had TRULY and UNDENIABLY just gone on a date. A real date-y date, like the kind you read about in those old-fashioned books. Which meant that I hadn't hallucinated all this weirdness between us.

GIVE ME A
118!

He really must feel the same way about me that I do about him!!! Right? **HOW INSANE IS THAT?!** I mean, it would still be cool if he actually told me out loud that he liked me, so there would be no question about it. But it is still kind of fun, I think, having to wonder just a little bit.

Now I'm sitting on my bed, replaying the night over and over. I'm wearing my pj's now, but I haven't taken the bangle off because it reminds me of how just a little while ago, Evan Andrews was holding MY hand. And it DEFINITELY wasn't an accident.

GIVE ME A 119!

Saturday, April 23

After the art gallery

Spirit Level:

Flashing a cheer-worthy smile

This morning I woke up with the biggest grin on my face. I still wanted to pinch myself to make sure I hadn't dreamed up the whole date with Evan, but when I looked at the bangle on my wrist (which I was **STILL** wearing), I knew it had been real. Can someone say **BLISSED OUT?**

Still bleary-eyed from sleep, I touched one of the keys on my keyboard to wake up my computer and see if maybe, just maybe, Evan had left me a cute message. Something like, "Had fun last night!" or "Hope you slept well!" but unforch, all I had was a message from Katarina asking, "Madison, what to be wearing for competition? Packing is now." Talk about being a tad over-prepared.

I tried not to let the lack of a follow-up note from Evan get me down. I had a big day ahead. A day with

GIVE ME A 120!

Katie and Luc! How bizarre. But also kind of fun! I don't go to the city that often, so it was kind of a big deal. And to not have to worry about taking public transportation there (read: MAJOR DRAG) was the icing on the cake (though the fact that this meant riding in a car with Ed Datner and Mom made that a slightly icky-tasting icing).

At least we were driving somewhere where it wasn't really likely someone from school would see us all together.

Dressing to meet up with Katie and Luc was only a little less difficult than dressing for my date with Evan. Number one, I had to look "city chic" and number two, well . . . There was no number two. Let's face it: I didn't want to look like a dork around Luc. His world probably looks like an Urban Outfitters catalog 24/7.

One of my purchases from my New York trip fit the bill—a silky button-down empire-waist dress with riding boots that I got near Canal Street.

I heard the doorbell ring, which meant Mr. D was here.

"Maaaads! You ready?" Mom called from downstairs.

"One sec!" I shouted. I quickly called to Lanie to wish me luck with the very strange day I had ahead of me.

GIVE ME A 121!

"Sounds like you don't need it, after last night's story," she quipped. When I'd called her last night to tell her about the date, she said her jaw was literally on the floor as I was describing Evan's hand-holding move. "I just have trouble picturing Evan as a romantic. But hey, I guess you really never know a person!"

"Believe me, I'm still surprised at how I'M acting around Evan," I said with a laugh.

"Hey, Madison!" Mom shouted again. She usually wasn't a nervous Nellie, but driving into the city wasn't her favorite. She hated all the traffic. I hoped Mr. D would help calm her nerves a bit, though.

"Coming!" I shouted back, quickly spraying myself with my fave raspberry spritz.

"Whoa, Mads. Bust a girl's eardrums, why don't ya?" said Lanie.

"Sorry," I said. "Later!"

I took one last look in the mirror and jetted downstairs.

Once we were in the car, Mr. D started his attempt at Awkward Adult to Kid Conversation.

"So, Madison. Anything new at school?"

Uhhhh. If I was answering honestly, I'd be like, "Yeah! My former best friend and I went on a date last night, and also, there's a super-mean cheerleader

GIVE ME A
122!

who seems like she's out to get me." As if. What did he really expect me to say?

"No, not really," I answered him.

"Madison," said Mom encouragingly. "Tell him about Get Up and Cheer! Or the fair."

"Oh, yeah," I said. "We have a pretty-big-deal competition coming up."

"Really?" said Mr. Datner, turning around in his seat to look at me. "The Grizzlies?"

"It's a novice competition, but yeah." It was a little hard for me to hide the frustration in my voice. What did he think, that the Grizzlies couldn't stand a chance in any competition?

"They're gonna be super," said Mom with a cheery smile. "They amaze me more and more each day." At least she was sticking up for me. But this, I realized, was the moment for Ye Olde iPod to save the day.

"You guys mind if I listen to some music?" I said.

Mom instantly went to the dial of the radio.

"No, I meant, I'm just gonna zone out for a bit back here."

"Oh. Of course, sweetie, go ahead."

I listened to the Get Up and Cheer! playlist and reviewed some of the choreography in my head. Man, did we look good in my imagination!

GIVE ME A
123!

When we pulled up to the gallery, Mom told me that she and Mr. D were going to make a day of being in the city, and just to call her "whenever." Score! Even though we didn't plan on leaving the gallery, I was psyched to have a couple of hours with friends in the city. Ah, the sweet smell of freedom. This was shaping up to be not such a bad weekend. (And by not so bad, I mean, UH-MAZING.)

The gallery was WAY smaller than I imagined it would be from the pictures. Which meant it wasn't the best place to be "secretive," since if you so much as sneezed, the entire room would know. I just crossed my fingers we wouldn't see anyone we knew. Besides, what were the chances? Of all the places to hang out in the entire city, it would be strange if someone from school just happened to be there too. (Unless they're one of the art geeks at school, who walk around wearing berets and talking about words that strictly end in "ism.")

As soon as you walk into the gallery, there's a big sign that says "EXIT" in block letters that look like decals someone stuck there. At first I was confused, because I thought it meant maybe I was entering the wrong way. Then I realized that there was a price tag next to it. Of course. This was one of the "art pieces."

GIVE ME A 124!

Four thousand buckaroos! Whoa. That's some expensive decal!

I found Luc in line by the café, but his back was to me. His hair had grown in where it had been shaved, and he'd dyed the tips of it a deep red. He was wearing a superthin, almost gauzy black T-shirt with a too-small hoodie that had a picture of a bleeding rose and some band name on it. I walked right up to him to make sure it was actually him before I shouted "Hey, Luc" or anything like that. Maybe he has Maddy Radar, because as soon as I got up close, he happened to turn to face me.

"Hey!" I said. "I thought that was you. I just wasn't sure. . . ."

He ran a hand through his hair. "Yeah, I should have warned you guys about my 'new look.'" He smiled.

"It's cool!" I said.

"Thanks." He reached out to give me a hug, which I wasn't expecting. And since I wasn't expecting it, as he came toward me I instinctively walked backward a step and heard a loud "Ouch!" behind me as I stepped on some lady's toe.

"Oops! I'm so sorry," I said to the woman. She just sneered at me and walked off with her cappuccino. Then, realizing (a little too late) that Luc had gone in

GIVE ME A
125!

for a hug, I went to give him one. But by now it was really awkward, and the timing was all off.

He laughed but hugged me anyway. "Spazzy much?"

"That's actually one of my nicknames. Spazzmadstic Madison. Sorry about that." I blushed. I don't know what it is about this guy, but he makes me nervous. Not in a "heart fluttery" kind of way (okay, maybe it was a little like that when I saw him in New York), but just in a "don't know how to be comfortable around him" kind of way. Maybe because he's so different from anyone we know in Port Angeles?

"That's hilarious," he said. We had gotten to the front of the line. "You eating anything?"

"Um . . ." I scanned the chalkboard that listed the specials of the day but decided to go with what I'd read online. "Yeah. I think the Death by Chocolate cake sounds good."

"Cool."

He placed both our orders with the barista, but thankfully there was no awkward "who should pay" business. Because, of course, this wasn't a date! I looked around toward the entrance (er, "exit" if you go by the art on the wall) and saw that thankfully, Katie had arrived. She had definitely dressed up for the occasion too. Her outfit was unlike anything she'd wear

GIVE ME A 126!

to school (except the fact that it consisted of some fashion-forward items). She had on shiny black leggings and a long, loose, black-and-white-patterned top plus a sleeveless vest hanging over it and ankle booties. I had trouble imagining Katie Parker standing in front of her closet, worrying about what to wear to meet her friends in the city. But the possibility of that was kind of comforting, I have to admit. She spotted us immediately, her whole face breaking into one of her megawatt smiles. I swear the room got brighter for a moment.

"Maddy! Luc!" she said, tottering toward us on her stiltlike shoes. "I am SO sorry I'm late," she said. "The bus took FOREVER."

"You took the bus?" I said, feeling instantly guilty that I hadn't thought of offering her a ride. "You should have come with me. My mom drove."

"Aw, it's okay," she said. "My mom was supposed to drive me, but she got roped into some auction thingy. Whatever." She shrugged.

"Well, we can give you a ride back," I said, even though that meant Katie would know the real deal about my mom and Mr. D. But it was a sacrifice I was willing to make. What can I say? Sometimes I am more like Mother Teresa than I realize.

GIVE ME A 127!

Luc and I grabbed a table while Katie placed her order. When she came to sit with us, she had a slightly worried look on her face. "**NOW** I remember why this place sounded so familiar," she said, opening a sugar packet. "Clementine's family drags her here all the time. They're big art collectors."

I wanted to say, "Couldn't you have thought of that earlier?" We'd gone out of our way to pick a place no one would supposedly see us at, and of **COURSE** the one place I decide on happens to be a Prescott Family Hangout.

I looked around the tiny gallery. From where I was sitting, it looked like we were Clementine free. "The coast looks clear for now at least," I said.

Katie did a once-over on the place as well. "Well I'm gonna keep my eyes peeled either way. Running into her here would be Bad News Bears."

"Whoa," said Luc, turning his chair around so he could straddle it. "Who's this citrusy-sounding girl? Someone you guys don't like?"

I laughed. As strange as her name was, no one had ever described it that way. "Well . . . ," I said, not quite sure how to answer that.

"She's my best friend," said Katie, coming to the rescue. "But there's just some stuff we don't talk

GIVE ME A 128!

about." Her eyes quickly flicked to me. "stuff that she wouldn't understand."

Luc looked from me to Katie to me again. "I won't ask. But that's quite a strange best friend to have. I couldn't keep secrets from mine even if I wanted to."

"Must be a girl thing," Katie said, forcing a laugh. But I knew she was just trying to close the book on the subject.

we hung out at the table for a while, digging into our desserts and swapping them with one another. I have to say the chocolate cake won, hands down, as MVP of the dessert selections. I thought I caught Luc looking at me more than he looked at Katie, which made me kind of uncomfortable (see?). Although it would have been flattering, I didn't want this guy to have a crush on me or anything like that. I needed boy drama like I needed a ripped cheer uniform. I tried to figure out how I could slip the word "boyfriend" into the conversation (even though E and I are so not official) to make it clear that I was just looking for cake in this café, not a boyfriend. Then I remembered that when I'd first met Luc, he knew I had a boyfriend, but that didn't stop him from being flirty that time either. So I was ÜBER relieved when he brought up the subject of his "girl."

GIVE ME A 129!

Katie, never one to miss a beat on gossip, instantly perked up. "Ooh, tell us! Is it anyone I know?"

Luc shook his head and wiped a crumb from the side of his mouth. "Nah. She just transferred to school right after you guys went back to Port Angeles. She was in my drama class, and we had to work on a skit together. She's awesome." His smile got recognizably larger as he talked about her. I wondered if Evan looked like this when he talked about me.

And since by then it was clear that Luc was just being nice to me and not flirty (sidebar comment: Miss Madison Hays, why do you assume every guy on the planet has a thing for you?), I was able to just relax.

Katie came up with the fun idea that we should go around the gallery, imitate pieces of artwork, and make the other two people guess which piece it was. Sort of like an art charades. I couldn't help but think that this would have been totally dorky if I was the one who'd come up with the idea, but since Katie is the Queen of Cool (or one of three), it wasn't. It was fun to see Katie loosen up from her usual cool-girl act that she has at school. Maybe just taking her out of Port Angeles did the trick.

When it was Luc's turn, he said he needed a partner. I walked up to him, giggling and hoping that he wasn't

GIVE ME A 130!

about to imitate the piece that showed a chicken getting its head eaten by a bear (gross). Instead he put his arm around me. (And this time I wasn't freaked out, cuz I knew it was just friendly.) Katie scanned the room, looking for the piece that this was supposed to remind us of. I couldn't really turn because I was being used as "the prop." But from the corner of my eye I saw someone step out from behind one of the columns in the gallery, and I heard the telltale click of a camera phone.

"Miss! Excuse me, but please, no photography," chided one of the guards.

I turned to see who'd taken the picture but saw that the door to the gallery was already closing behind whoever had just dashed out of there. Totally weird, right?

"Ooh, someone got schooled," said Luc, looking toward the exit.

"I got it!" said Katie, oblivious to the commotion. "It's that one." She walked over to the piece that showed two genderless stick figures next to each other, one stick figure with its arms around the other. I could have drawn that in my sleep! I seriously should consider becoming an artist.

"Nice work," said Luc.

GIVE ME A 131!

I was going to bring up what had just happened, but then decided to just keep going with our game. WHY AM I BEING PARANOID? People must try to sneak pictures in galleries all the time. Just because someone took a picture somewhere NEAR me, didn't mean it was one OF me. First I think Luc is flirting with me, and now I am imagining that the paparazzi are stalking me. Seriously, I need to have a long talking-to with my ego.

After our gallery game, we took a walk around the block. Katie kept asking Luc, in various ways, how her dance friends from New York were doing. I don't know why she couldn't just come out and ask the question she wanted to ask (who of her friends got in where), but maybe she didn't want to seem nosy. So finally, I stepped in (cuz I'm so nice!) and said, "So, who made it in?"

Luc said that their friends Penelope and Darren made the cut, but Magda didn't.

Katie stopped in her tracks. "What? MAGDA didn't get in? But she was, like, the best dancer there. That's insane."

Luc nodded. "Yeah. Everyone's talking about how random the admissions selections were. There were amazing dancers who didn't get in, and not-so-amazing dancers who did. It didn't seem to always have to do that much with how good people were overall. Of course,

GIVE ME A 132!

there were also amazing dancers, like Penelope, who did get in."

"I guess," said Katie, frowning into the distance. "I just thought I would be one of those amazing dancers who WOULD get in." Then, realizing she'd just given herself a major compliment (hey, guess I'm not the only one), she quickly clasped her hand over her mouth. "Did I just say that out loud?"

Luc and I laughed. "It's okay," I said. "You ARE an amazing dancer."

"Honestly, everyone was surprised you didn't make it," Luc said.

"Thanks, guys," said Katie. "I know I decided in the end that I was going to stick with cheerleading no matter what, but it was a blow to my ego not to make the cut. You know? Sometimes I wish I could have it both ways."

After Katie said that, I realized that I am pretty lucky. I got to try out for what I thought was my dream team—and I made it! But I still decided in the end to stick with the Grizzlies. At least I had a choice in the matter.

My phone buzzed in my pocket. I hoped that it was a call from E, but the caller ID said "Coach," i.e., Mom. So much for being picked up "whenever."

GIVE ME A 133!

"Sweetie? We're actually in the neighborhood. Could we swing by in a few?"

"Sure," I said. "Um, can we take Katie Parker home too?"

"Oh, Katie?" I could tell Mom was surprised but was glad she didn't ask or say anything about it. Katie and I didn't usually hang out outside of school.

"Yeah, she was here too."

"Of course."

I put my phone back in my pocket. "Sorry, guys," I said. "Fun's over. My mom's swinging by the gallery any minute."

I still can't believe Katie's parents just let her take the bus into the city. I know her dad works a lot, and her mom does lots of volunteer work, but still. My mom would never let me go to the city by myself. I know Mom is overprotective, but that means I get a ride to and from places without having to inch through town at a snail's pace as we make all local stops.

It's funny: I always thought Katie had the perfect everything. But the more I get to know her, the more I realize how much more there is to learn about her.

We said good-bye to Luc, who was going to meet up with one of his cousins somewhere else in the city. "Call me the next time you guys are in New York!" he said,

GIVE ME A 134!

before flipping his hoodie over his head and walking away.

"We will!" Katie and I called after him in unison as we got into the car.

The ride back home was bearable. Mr. D and Mom luckily kept their hands to themselves (how mortifying would it have been if they'd held hands in the car?!?). I think I was kidding myself that absolutely no one knew about my mom and Mr. D being a couple. Katie didn't even flinch when she saw him in the car. She just said, "Oh, hey, Mr. D," like it was no big deal. Still, I could live without news of Mom and Mr. D's outing to the city being public knowledge. But I have a good hunch that Katie is going to keep this little piece of gossip to herself.

When I got home, I hopped onto my computer and FINALLY there was a little message from Evan. "I had a lot of fun the other night," it said. There wasn't much else, but that's okay. Yay! It wasn't just me who'd had a blast. Can't wait to see him at school tomorrow.

GIVE ME A 135!

Monday, April 25

Not-so-good morning at school

Spirit Level:

Plummeting from the Top of the Pyramid

OMG. UTTER DISASTER. I'm still trying to process what just happened. It was like a scene from out of my worst nightmare. Going insane right now!!! I know I'm supposed to get to class, but I feel like if I go there now, I'm going to just sit there with a shocked look on my face (like that poster in art class of the painting <u>The Scream</u>).

So here's the sitch: I went to see Evan before second period, and when I went up to him, he was staring at his cell phone, looking confused.

"Hey, you," I said. "Everything okay?"

He handed me his phone so I could see the message myself, his lips all crumpled into a puzzled frown. "Someone sent this pic to me just now. I thought you said you were going to sew what? on Saturday. Unless this is a friend you made in the knitting aisle."

GIVE ME A
136!

I knew what the pic would be before I even laid eyes on it. I suddenly flashed back to the moment in the gallery when I thought I heard someone taking a picture. Lo and behold, it was a pic of Luc and me, with his arm casually draped around me, with the date and time that the picture had been taken. My heart dropped. I shook my head in disbelief. Someone had sent this to Evan to make it look like I'd lied to him and was hanging out with a mystery boy. A mystery boy that I wouldn't be able to explain to Evan.

"So? What's the deal?" he asked shakily. He grabbed his phone back.

"I—I—" I didn't know what to say. I couldn't tell him the truth without having to explain EVERYTHING. About Katie, about the New York trip. Everything. "He's just a friend of mine," I said. I knew it sounded totally lame.

Evan just gave me a cold look. "Weird. You never mentioned him before. And why did you say you were going to be at Sew What? Why did you lie? I'm your, um, friend, right?"

A girl from my social studies class stared at us as we walked by, then scurried toward one of her friends and whispered in her ear. Clearly we were making the school-day drama list.

GIVE ME A 137!

I sighed, more out of frustration than anything. "I'm really sorry, but I can't tell you a lot about him. I promised another friend that I'd keep our friendship a secret." I know that sounds like the worst excuse ever, but what was I supposed to say? It was the truth. Or part of it.

Evan looked really confused. "who, Lanie?" he squeaked, his voice breaking slightly.

I shook my head. "I'm so sorry, but I can't say." I could literally feel his anger rippling off him, so I tried changing the subject. "want to wait for me after practice?" I asked, hoping his answer would be yes.

Evan practically stuttered his response. "I, uh—uh—no. I'm kind of busy tonight. So, um . . . later, Madison."

Before I could say anything, he was walking away with his shoulders hunched up practically to his ears.

I leaned against the wall and slid to the floor in misery. I couldn't imagine what Evan must be feeling. Like, we had this awesome date on Friday, and the next day there I was snuggling up to some strange guy. Just call me Two-Time Madison.

GIVE ME A 138!

WHY COULDN'T WHOEVER HAD TAKEN THE PICTURE HAVE SNAPPED IT WITH KATIE IN THE FRAME TOO?

That would have at least looked a little better. But that must have been the point, right? To make me look bad and to get me in trouble with Evan? And who in the world would have taken this picture? Why would whoever it was go out of her way to hurt me? Well, paging Captain Obvious. . . .

Who else could it be but a certain Clementine Prescott? Can't she find someone else to torment? How did I ever get to be so "lucky"? I preferred it before, when she barely knew who I was and just gave me the same dirty looks she gave everyone. Now she's PLAYING DIRTY.

I decided to write Katie a quick note and slip it into her locker. "We need to talk," it said.

I'm done with keeping Katie's secrets. Evan needs to know the truth about this picture, and I don't care if it means Katie might be on the outs with Clementine as a result. How did it end up that Katie's stupid secrets are ruining my LIIIIIIIFE?

Ugh. Principal G approaching. Gotta get to class. PLEASE LET THIS DAY END SOON!!!

GIVE ME A 139!

LATER THAT NIGHT, SOAKING MY SORROWS IN THE TUB

So obviously I had a little trouble focusing during practice today. I was a total space cadet during our entire warm-up. Evan was nowhere to be seen at lunch, and when I walked past him in the hallway, he completely IGNORED me. Why do I feel like every moment we get somewhere good, something happens to totally take us off track? Lanes listened patiently as I whined to her about my situation, and she agrees it is time to say something to Katie.

"You can't keep Katie's secret if it means hurting yourself. Or other people, like Evan," she said.

I knew she was right. But I wanted to talk to Katie first before I did anything rash. What a DILEMMA.

Jacqui, thank goodness, could read my warning signs at the beginning of practice (or make that panic signs), so she picked up most of the slack today (I heart that gurrrrl).

During practice, Mom asked everyone to sit tight as she explained the logistics of the Get Up and Cheer! competition (the least fun part of a competition, in my book). I forced myself to snap out of my funk and go into my captain mode.

GIVE ME A 140!

"Everyone needs to be in the school parking lot, ready to board the buses, by six a.m.," said Mom in her matter-of-fact voice. "No stragglers, okay, guys?"

Cue groans from nearly every person on the team. "But Coach," said Jared, "the competition doesn't start until ten, right?"

Mom shook her head. "People start competing at ten, but we have to first get ourselves assembled here, then who knows what kind of traffic we'll have, and once we get to the site we have to register. And since we won't know what order we're competing in until we get there, we need to be prepared to go first."

I knew Mom would get totally OCD about this competition. She's always told me how on her own competition days, she'd get up with the roosters and start warming her body up. Then she'd have her mom drive her to the competitions before anyone else (not even the janitor) arrived, so she could "visualize herself on the mat." It all sounded like a nice idea, and I even tried to do it a couple of times (and by try, I mean, I set my alarm clock and hit snooze a dozen times). But the reality of depriving myself of beauty sleep always won out.

GIVE ME A 14!!

"I'm going to be a zombie!" Jared whined.

"Not if you go to bed early at least two nights before, to prepare," Mom chided.

Jared moaned, but he knew he wouldn't win this battle. Not when it came to Coach Carolyn.

"Come on, guys, let's get psyched!" said Jacqui. "It's our first real competition EVER! Who cares if we lose a few z's?"

"She's right," I said. "We've been looking forward to this for, like, ever."

"Yeah," said Tabitha Sue. "It'll be fun, just us Grizzlies on the bus. I'll bring homemade protein bars!"

Mom held a finger up to signal that she had more to say. "Well, it will mainly just be us Grizzlies, but we do need to have another chaperone."

I prayed that this plan wouldn't involve Mr. Datner. Just what I needed, the two of them holding hands across the aisle while everyone made fun of me. I could even hear the songs they'd sing along the way: "Coach Carolyn and Mr. Datner sitting in a tree . . ."

"Coach Whipley has kindly agreed to accompany us on the trip."

I wasn't so sure that Coach Whipley was that much of an improvement over Mr. D. If anything, she was probably worse.

GIVE ME A
142!

A chorus of moans went up in protest, louder than when Mom had announced our early meeting time. Just seeing Coach Whipley in the gym sent shots of anxiety through everyone's brains. She was an awesome coach (if having a winning team is what makes you awesome), yeah, except that her coaching method relied more on fear than anything else. I think the Titans jump as high as they do because if they didn't, she'd make them land on a bed of spikes or something.

"And," said Mom, ignoring the reaction from the team, "Coach Whipley will be asking one Titan to come with her as an assistant for the day."

This time, the moans and groans were even louder. I held back from joining them, even though inside I was like, "Noooo!" Unless it was Katie, having a Titan at OUR competition—the one we'd worked so hard for—would definitely ruin the mood of the day.

"If we'd wanted the Titans to be there, we would have sent out a handwritten invitation," said Jared.

"Wait. Which Titan?" asked Jacqui. I was glad that she was the one to ask the question that was on my lips. I didn't want to get one of my mom's "looks" for not being a "team player."

Mom shrugged her shoulders. "She hasn't told me yet. But who cares, kids?" she said with her "go team

GIVE ME A
143!

go!" smile. "We all represent Port Angeles, and Titan or Grizzly, we're on the same team. It is really nice that the Titans want to give us part of their weekend to help us out."

Yeah. "Nice." I didn't have a good feeling about this new development.

After practice I pulled Mom aside. "Really? Coach Whipley?" I asked. I knew I shouldn't have shown her that I was annoyed, but I couldn't help it.

"Sweetie, I thought you'd be happy I didn't ask Ed. I was trying to be considerate of your feelings."

I instantly felt bad that Mom had done this for me, and here I was being ungrateful. It was nice of her to think about how the idea of everyone seeing her and Mr. D together might make me feel. But still. Coach Whipley? Shiver.

Lanie came over earlier tonight and lay on my bed listening to me whine for an hour before we got down to business. T-shirt-designing business, that is. She asked me if I'd spoken to Katie yet, but I hadn't been able to. Practice had run late, and the Titans were in the middle of some deep discussion by the time I left the locker room. Le sigh.

I hadn't heard from Evan, either, but I wasn't surprised after how we left things. Well, not THAT

GIVE ME A
144!

surprised. Of course I was hoping he'd be waiting outside the gym, look up at me with his mopey eyes, and say, "I'm sorry we had a fight. I trust you. If you don't want to talk about the picture, it's NBD."

YEAH, RIGHT. In my dreams.

After I complained for the hundredth time about how horrible it was to see Evan so mad at me, Lanie turned to me and said, "Okay. I'm going to say this one time, and don't be mad."

I nodded okay.

"I think you need to stop worrying about being such a good friend to Katie, and more about being good to yourself."

"But Lanes, I wouldn't do that to you. If you needed me to keep a secret, I would, no matter what."

"Yeah, but I would never make you keep a secret like that. Not if it was hurting you to keep it."

I picked at the little balls of lint on the Peter Rabbit doll that had been on my bed since before I could remember. "Yeah, yeah," I said, not really wanting to agree with her out loud. Even though inside, I knew she had a really good point.

Then Lanie sat up straight, put a hand over her heart, and started bouncing on the bed. "I hereby declare that from now on tonight, we are going to talk

GIVE ME A
145!

about anything and everything BUT Katie, Evan, or Clementine. Deal?" she asked, holding out a hand for me to shake.

That sounded really good to me. I grabbed her hand. "Deal."

We spent the rest of the night eating Twizzlers while making posters for the booth and finalizing some designs. It was nice to get my mind off things, even though it was only for a little while.

After she left, though, I started obsessing over everything again. I started to think that maybe Lanie was right. I feel like I've told Katie lots of times how keeping this secret is making me feel, and how it would be better for everyone (okay, maybe just me) if she came clean. But she hasn't budged at all. It's kind of not fair. I was thinking of just picking up the phone and calling Evan to tell him everything (assuming he'd answer my call), and practically right at the moment when I was dialing his number in my cell, my phone rang. I didn't recognize the number and thought for a millisecond that maybe HE was calling ME from a weird number so he could hear my voice and hang up. My brain was def on overdrive tonight.

"Hello?"

"Hey, Madison, it's Katie."

GIVE ME A 146!

Whoa. Does she have some kind of ESP?

She immediately launched into apology mode. "Sorry we didn't get to talk earlier. I wanted to go over to you, but we were getting an old-fashioned Whipley whipping about dress code. Hope you don't mind me calling so late."

I was sure there was more to that story, and ordinarily I would have been all over Katie, asking who had broken code, and what Whipley had said. But I was too annoyed about other things.

"No, not at all. So," I said, stalling a little, "the reason I wrote you that note was because of . . . Listen, I think Clementine did something."

Katie was quiet for a few beats, but then she asked, "Way to be cryptic, Madison. Like what? What do you mean?"

I told her all about that moment in the gallery when I heard the camera phone click, and how there was a commotion with one of the security guards there. "I tried to see who'd gotten caught snapping a photo, but whoever it was had already disappeared. It was weird, though, because I had a feeling at the time that the pic wasn't just of one of the art pieces there."

"So why didn't you say anything?" said Katie.

"I don't know. I didn't want you guys to think I was

GIVE ME A 147!

being paranoid. But that's not the whole story," I said. I continued to explain what had happened earlier today, with Evan and the picture that was sent to him and how he wouldn't even talk to me now.

"Oh. My. God," said Katie. "You think it was Clementine?" Her voice sounded a little like it was coming from the other side of a door, kind of muffled and sad. I felt AWFUL about pointing a finger at her friend, but wasn't it obvious?

"Katie," I said, "you're the one who told me that Clem goes to that gallery all the time with her fam."

"I know Clem has her bad moments, but it's just hard for me to think she would do something THAT mean." I could tell by the sound of her voice that maybe it wasn't that hard for her to imagine Clem doing something like this, but it definitely was hard to swallow.

"What, do you think that I have, like, multiple enemies at school?" I asked. I was feeling a little frustrated. Who else would have tried to ruin my relationship with Evan? It certainly wasn't Mr. Hobart.

Katie didn't say anything for a few seconds. "Madison, the thing is, I tried to talk to her the other day about the way she's been acting toward you."

This was news. I'd thought Katie had given up trying

GIVE ME A 148!

to defend me to her BFF. "Oh," I said. "You did?"

"Yeah. But she got all up on my case, and was like, 'Ooh, sorry. Didn't mean to offend your new best friend. Should we go bake her Funfetti cupcakes?'"

"Okay," I said. "So then what did you say?" I was hoping maybe she'd taken that opportunity to tell Clem the whole truth about auditions, New York, and everything.

"I just couldn't, Madison. I tried, but I couldn't."

It was exactly as I'd suspected. Katie was too chicken to tell her friend the truth.

"Katie . . ."

"I know, I know!" said Katie, her voice rising. "I know how Clem gets, especially when she feels anxious or out of control. But I also know that she has her reasons for doing things. Like at first I thought she was just stressed about the fair and things with her mom. But now I think it's something else. Especially since she's getting worse and worse. I just can't figure out what that something else is." She sighed loudly into the phone. "But she's definitely got a sore spot with you, that's for sure."

"Yeah, no kidding." I was glad that Katie was finally seeing that this wasn't all just Clem being Clem. This was personal.

GIVE ME A 149!

"The thing is, I just don't think her beef with you could be ALL about you not becoming a Titan. Even for Clem, I feel like this is going too far. But if it's not that, then I just have no idea what she's so angry about."

I shrugged, even though Katie couldn't see me through the phone. "I wish I knew. Why don't you just ask her what's going on?"

"Yeah, Captain Obvious. Like she'd just come out and tell me. This is Clem we're talking about. She's the Queen of Avoiding the Issue."

"Yeah, I've experienced that firsthand."

"This is just awful," said Katie. "I feel like I'm causing problems for everyone. But Maddy, you have to still promise you won't say anything? Not even to Evan? I'm not ready to fess up. I know I'm being a total loser about this, but I'm sorry."

If she had called me maybe a few hours before, I might have put my foot down and said, "No, you HAVE to say something." But since Lanie had mellowed me out a little, I was easier to persuade. I guess it was a slight improvement that at least Katie could see that this thing with Clem was real.

"Okay," I agreed. (Though not happily.)

So now, just as I was about to tell Evan everything,

GIVE ME A 150!

there I was getting guilt-tripped again into still keeping this stupid secret. I hate the way things are with Evan and me right now, but what can I do? I don't want to betray Katie. I think I'll give this secret thing a little more time, but honestly I don't know how much longer I can keep this going.

Just went online to see if Evan is there.

His screen name said he was active, so I mustered all the courage I had and sent him a message. "Heyyyy Evan. u therrre?"

Of course, nothing. Well, I figured, I couldn't tell him the truth, but I could at least try to explain things to him.

"E, I'm really sry. I kno it looks like I lied 2 u, but I SWEAR it isn't what u thinkkk. Just trust me, okay? I promise 2 tell u everything as soon as I possibly can. I HATE how things r btwn us rite now."

I pressed send, and then checked back every five seconds to see if he'd responded. But the only e-mail I got was from Lanes, and it was a pic of one of the T-shirt designs we'd talked about earlier (a supercute one, BTW. It had a halter neck and little slits up the sides, fastened with safety pins). Yeah, it was a good message, but not the one I'd been hoping for. Sigh.

I know I shouldn't have done this, but I couldn't help

GIVE ME A 151!

it. I sent E one more message before shutting down for the night. If I didn't physically turn my computer off, then I could totally see myself staying up all night to check if he'd written me back.

"G'nite E" was all it said.

I waited a full minute, but still nothing.

So now I'm taking a "long soak in the tub," as Mom likes to say. Like in the movies, you always see stressed-out women in tubs with candles and a washcloth over their eyes. It always looks so soothing, like all their problems will go away with this tub. For me, not so much. Though I did try out a lavender bubble bath sample from Mom's cabinet that was pretty groovy. A girl's got to find her bright side somewhere, right?

GIVE ME A 152!

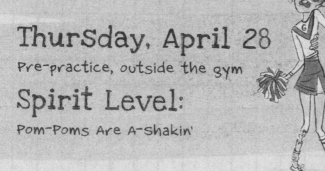

Thursday, April 28
Pre-practice, outside the gym
Spirit Level:
Pom-Poms Are A-Shakin'

Just have a teeny-tiny second to write because I've been in **CRAZY CHEER** prep mode. Thank goodness I have Get Up and Cheer! to think about, because things with Evan have gone from worse to even **MORE** worse (is that even a saying?). Every time I see him in school he looks pretty down in the dumps, and he **NEVER** responded to any of my texts or e-mails. Lanie said she tried talking to him about it, but he just said he didn't feel like talking about it. (That was nice of her, though.) I'm, like, this close to decorating his locker with cutout paper hearts and delivering flowers to his classroom door, begging forgiveness and understanding. But luckily, I'm not that much of a dork.

I've lost both a cute crush and a best friend. I hate going through this really stressful precompetition week without having E to complain to. Poor Lanie has

GIVE ME A 153!

had to hear it all a million times because there's NO ONE ELSE! Katie's been too much in her own world too, because the Titans have, like, a million games coming up. So I haven't had a chance to check in and see if maybe she'd changed her mind about telling Clem her secret (like she would have changed her mind in a day, anyway). Meanwhile Clementine has this big ol' smile on her face every time she sees me in the hall. Like she couldn't be happier with the way things are: Me, unhappy and Evan-less. Her, Queen of Everything: from running the fair to ruining my life.

Mom even canceled her "date night" with Mr. D to hang with me tonight because she could tell I was upset. I don't want to go into my boy problems with her (gross), but at least it was nice that she is trying to be understanding. Even if her version of understanding usually has to do with stuffing me with pizza and junk food, and then making us watch her old cheer videos. Aw, good ol' Mom. She means well, I guess.

But back to the competition: I'm feeling pretty good about this. Our pyramid is looking SUPERFINE (no one has toppled over!) and we're getting the timing of everything right. We made a video of the routine, and we hit it almost perfectly (though I need to work on cleaning up my round-offs a little). Even the Beyoncé

GIVE ME A 154!

moves are lookin' hawt. Mom is super psyched for us.
She's even promised a bagel breakfast for the morning
of the competition, to get everyone revved up.

Here's the big plus:

The rest of the Grizzlies seem psyched too, and no
one has said a peep about the Diane thing in forever. I
think what really helps this team is when they believe
in themselves (cheesy, but true). Once they have a
good attitude about what they're going to do, the rest
just seems to fall into place. The opposite is true too:
If they start feeling nervous about something, the
mistakes pile up one on top of another like dominoes.
Not good.

Tomorrow night we're taking our first night off
from practice in what seems like ages, so we can rest
up for the big day on Saturday. Actually, it's going to be
quite a big weekend in general. We have the competition
on Saturday and the fair on Sunday. I'm going to be a
walking zombie on Monday.

Seriously, my whole body hurts from practicing too
much. Jacqui made us do a billion squats and lunges to
really "power up those legs." I feel like I'm in such good
shape, though. That's one of the things I really like
about competitions: They push you to work yourself
to the edge until everything looks perfect. And really,

GIVE ME A
155!

in cheer, there's no room for mistakes. (That's what I leave my regular life for. Ha-ha.)

Oh, I never wrote what the cheer part of our routine is:

GRIZZLIES!

GO GRIZZLIES!

WE'RE RISING TO THE TOP.

AND WHEN WE GO TO THE TOP

WE HIT IT AND DON'T STOP.

GRIZZLIES ROAR,

"GIVE ME MORE!"

GRIZZLIES ROAR

"GIVE ME MORE!"

SLASHING THROUGH THE CEILING

HEAR THE GRIZZLIES ROAR!

Cute, right? I don't care that during practice when we were screaming our lungs out, some of the Titans started laughing. I think they're just trying to psych us out. Not like we're competing against THEM or anything, but I guess they're just bad sports. Most of them, anyway.

K, wish me luck!

Gooooo Grizzlies!

GIVE ME A 156!

Saturday, April 30

On the bus ride home

Spirit Level:

We Got It in the Bag!

SO MUCH TO WRITE ABOUT!

This morning already feels like forever ago. I woke up to the smell of freshly ironed cheer uniform. YUM! Mom likes to iron my cheer uniforms the night before, AND the morning of, just in case a tiny wrinkle may have made its way into the skirt. She's nuts about stuff like that. Of course she was up before the sun and STILL managed to look like she'd had twenty hours of sleep. How does she do that? I am so not a morning person.

I was still half-asleep when we got into the car to drive over to school. I rolled down all the windows and blasted the music on high.

"Maddy," said Mom. "Get your head in the game. You want to set a good example for the rest of the team,

GIVE ME A 157!

don't you? And here, put this in your bag for later." She handed me a Tupperware of boiled eggs.

I knew she was right about me getting into the game. I tried to focus and bring as much pep into my system as possible. I pictured energetic things like jumping into a pool of cold water, running through a finish line, and most important of all: winning first place at a cheer competition. Suddenly, my nerves kicked in. What if we fall flat on our faces during the pyramid? What if someone twists her ankle during a tumbling sequence? And that's when I realized: Nerves are a great way to stay awake and focused!!!

You know what else can snap a girl into attention mode? Seeing your arch nemesis boarding the bus to YOUR most important competition of the year. So, yeah, I couldn't believe my eyes when we pulled up to the school parking lot and saw Clementine standing there next to Coach Whipley. Guess that was my answer to the question of whom Whipley would nominate to be her assistant for the day. Clementine didn't look very thrilled to be there. I guessed either she'd agreed to help her coach with something without even knowing what it was (totally kiss-up-style), or she decided to come so that she could make my life even worse than it was already but hated having to give up a Saturday

GIVE ME A
158!

for it (awww, poor Clem. Not!). Turns out, though, that I was wrong on both guesses as to why Clem was in such a bad mood (more in a sec).

Mom dropped me off at the curb while she went and parked. Jacqui came running up to me, her dark curls bouncing up and down.

"Whoa, where's the fire?" I asked. "Is something wrong?"

"Everything's fine," said Jacqui. Then she looked behind her, then left, then right. "But listen, as you probably can see, Clem's coming along for the day." Jacqui rolled her eyes. "Girlie is in a bad way. She and her mom were literally screaming at one another when they pulled up. Even Coach Whipley tried to calm her down after her mom left. You could hear them yelling from, like, a mile away."

"Weird. I wonder what they were fighting about?"

Jacqui shook her head. "I have no idea. But if we had to worry about having an annoyed Clem with us before, now we have to worry about having an annoyed and ANGRY Clem. Trust me, from experience, the combo is not a good one."

"When is that girl ever NOT angry?"

Jacqui smiled. "I guess you're right. But today she seems more peeved than usual. Oh man, I hope

GIVE ME A 159!

Coach Whipley knew what she was doing in asking her to tag along."

Just then, Tabitha Sue came running over to us. "Hey, guys! You ready for our big day?" She was in high spirits, thank goodness. Her cheeks were flushed from sprinting to us, and her eyes had a little sparkle in them.

"More than ready," I replied.

"Ready to kick butt!" said Jacqui.

"Well, come on then and get on the bus! We're doing makeup."

I decided I would do my best to try and ignore Clem and her Mama Drama and enjoy just hanging with my team and getting psyched up with them. Katarina had brought what looked like a duffel bag purely devoted to makeup and beauty.

Jacqui got elbow-deep into the bag, seeing what goodies lay inside. "Seriously, Katarina? Six different types of hot rollers?"

"Of course," Katarina scoffed. "Everyvon has theee different hairs. Vich von vould like me to style zem?" She looked at Tabitha Sue, Jacqui, and me. Then her eyes landed on Jared.

"Hey, count me out!" said Jared. "My hair looks just fine the way it is."

GIVE ME A
160!

"Oh, come on, Jared," Tabitha Sue teased. "How about a little stage makeup?"

Jared covered his face with his hands. "No! No makeup. Ew!" He ducked behind the seat where Ian and Matt sat, listening to their iPods. "Guys, you have to help me. The Mary Kay ladies are attacking!"

Matt lowered his headphones. "Mary WHO?"

Jacqui passed around blue ribbons to all the girls. "These are good luck ribbons," she said. "To tie in our hair. Guess it's a Titan ritual I can't shake. Except the Titans always tie them in their laces."

"Nice. Thanks, Jacqui," I said.

Suddenly we were overcome with the smell of fresh bagels. I looked toward where the smell was coming from, and it was at the front of the bus, where Mom had been chatting with Coach Whipley. I didn't remember Mom bringing bagels into the car.

That's when I looked outside the bus and saw Mr. Datner driving off. I guess it was pretty nice of him to supply us with our morning carb fix.

"I promised you guys breakfast, and here it is!" she said, handing the bagels back. "We've got all flavors. There's low-fat cream cheese and butter in the bag. Don't ruin your uniforms!" She passed the bag to Clementine first, who was sitting in the front with

GIVE ME A 16!!

Mom and Whipley. Clementine frowned and wrinkled her nose. "Ugh. No thanks."

"What? They're still warm. Come on, have one," Mom said.

"No thanks, Coach Hays, I don't like to fill up on carbs. I have my protein shake in the cooler. So many less calories," she said smugly.

I knew Mom wanted to say something back to her but was holding it in. Mom was all about healthy eating, but she also knew that carbs aren't the worst thing before an action-packed day. "Suit yourself," she said, passing the bag to the Testosterone Twins instead.

As we were chowing down, Mom came toward the back of the bus and started counting heads. "Everyone here?" she said, counting one more time.

"No!" joked Ian.

Mom smiled. "Really funny."

She gave the bus driver the go-ahead to leave, and we started pulling out of the parking lot. "Okay, guys, this is it!" said Jacqui. "The moment we've all been waiting for. Who wants to sing some Grizzly songs?"

Clementine scowled and put her fingers in her ears.

I secretly wished that Clem and her Big Bad Mood had stayed at home. Even Mr. Datner would have been way better than this!

GIVE ME A 162!

It took a couple of hours, but we passed the time pretty well, singing songs and telling funny cheer stories. When we pulled up to the school where the competition was being held, people were bursting to get off the bus and find out where we'd be placed in the order of schools competing.

"All right, Grizzlies. Stick together!" said Mom. "Don't forget your stuff."

The school's gym was larger than ours, but way smaller than the one where the Titans had competed for Regional Qualifier. Still, it was all gussied up for competition day. There was a big stage in the middle of the auditorium that held the mat, with giant fluorescent lights that gave the mat an eerie glow. It was like the mat itself had some kind of supernatural power. I hoped it was the power to make us win.

You could smell the anticipation in the room. Cheerleaders wearing every color of the rainbow flipped, kicked, and cartwheeled across the mat. "Higher!" yelled one coach, who looked like she hadn't slept in years. "Did I say lower? I didn't think so. Girls, come on!" One of the cheerleaders ran off the mat in tears.

It's always moments like these when I'm happy that Mom is our coach. Her style is definitely serious and

GIVE ME A
163!

firm, but she doesn't put us down or make us feel bad.

I looked around at the competition and felt a little overwhelmed. Nearly every cheerleading team had its game face on. These girls looked FIERCE. Even though the competition was definitely a big deal for all the teams there that day (including us), I didn't expect everyone to look so serious. This was Get Up and Cheer!, not Regionals. I looked at Jacqui to see what she was feeling, and her face was just a sea of calm. I guess she's been to quite a few of these things in her life—and after having had to sub for Marissa at the Titans' Regional Qualifier, this probably seemed like a piece of cake.

Mom went off to register our team, so Jacqui and I went about finding a somewhat quiet corner to gather in a circle and stretch out for a bit. Until we knew when we were set to compete, we didn't want to tire the team out too fast.

When we sat down, I saw that Katarina was fidgeting with her bows nervously.

"What's wrong?" I asked.

"I am just sinking about Diane. She should be being here. She vas good flier. Good stunter."

I was like, "Oh no. Not the Diane stuff again . . ."

"Who?" said Jared. "I do not know this person thou

GIVE ME A
164!

speakest of. That name is dead to me."

I knew he wasn't still **THAT** upset over the Diane thing, because he hadn't talked about it in a while. That was probably his way of closing the conversation. Unfortunately, Katarina completely misunderstood and started freaking out.

"Vat? Diane ees not dead!"

"No, no," said Jared, laughing. "It's an expression."

Katarina exhaled with relief. "I am sorry. I have zee nerves."

Tabitha Sue patted Katarina on the back. "Don't worry, we're gonna rock this place."

"Of zis I hope," said Katarina.

We led the team through a series of stretches, and then Jacqui suggested we hold hands and "focus on ourselves winning." I've never been much into that "Kumbaya"-type stuff, but I figured it couldn't hurt.

When Ian and Matt finally stopped sniggering about how cheesy it was for all of us to hold hands (basically after Jacqui shot Matt one of her quieting looks), we all took a few deep breaths together.

"Now, envision yourself doing the routine," said Jacqui.

I opened my eyes just a bit to make sure that everyone was going along with this and was surprised

GIVE ME A 165!

to find the entire team's eyes were closed. Nice!

"Okay, we're totally synchronized. We're smiling, we're loud, we're full of energy."

I nodded, then realized that no one could see me agreeing with her.

When Jacqui was done, I could almost see the positive energy radiating from our team. We totally need to do this more often!

Mom came back and told us that we would be competing smack-dab in the middle of the day. I thought that was pretty good—it would give us time to prepare but not TOO much time. We waited for our turn on the practice mats, trying not to get psyched out by the other teams.

One team, the Hornets, wearing gold-and-black uniforms that literally seemed to sparkle, looked really awesome on the mat. There was one part where the team separated into three groups, and the bases lifted up the fliers at exactly the same moment. The fliers then did some heel-stretches into tick-tocks without missing a beat. They came down in a cradle, with huge smiles on their faces. This squad was definitely not boring.

"Wow," Mom whispered to me. "I think that's the competition."

"No kidding," I said.

GIVE ME A
166!

Finally it was our turn on the mat.

"Grizzlies!" said Mom. "You worked hard for this. You've gotten this far. This is your time to shine. Now show everyone what makes the Grizzlies roar!"

We ran onto the mat screaming as if this were the real deal, and not a practice run.

We tried to imagine our music, and as we began I could see Mom smiling at us from across the mat. Everything was going fine in the routine, from everyone remembering their places, to hitting each move with precision. And then a mini disaster struck: Tabitha Sue lost her balance in the middle of a heel-stretch and nearly ate the mat, before Ian caught her.

This was not a good sign. I knew it wouldn't take much to rattle Tabitha Sue. She gets so stressed out at these kinds of things, and I could tell that from the moment we'd entered the auditorium, she'd been a little on edge.

"Tabitha Sue, you okay?" I asked.

Her face looked white as she bent down to massage her leg. "This is bad, Madison. I never mess up that heel-stretch. What if this means I'm gonna mess up for real when we're out there?"

"Tabitha Sue," I said, "that's not gonna happen. This is what the run-throughs are for—you have to get all

GIVE ME A 167!

the bad stuff out here so only the good stuff happens when it's our turn."

"Did you hurt yourself?" asked Mom. A little wrinkle of worry appeared between her eyebrows.

"Not really. I mean, it hurts a little . . . ."

"I'm gonna go get you an ice pack. Rest it off, okay?" said Mom.

Tabitha Sue nodded.

"All right, guys, we're gonna continue our run-through without Tabitha Sue," Jacqui announced. This would be a real test for us—could we do the routine with a missing person?

The answer, thank goodness, was YES. The stunt sequence went off without a hitch. Tabitha Sue cheered her heart out from the sidelines.

"That looked awesome!" she said, as we came running off the mat, nearly everyone out of breath.

"Yeah?" I asked.

"Definitely," said Tabitha Sue. "Maybe you guys should do this without me."

I wasn't exactly sure she was being sarcastic, so I punched her in the shoulder. "Shut up! Please. Are you kidding me?"

"Hey, hey, just putting it out there," she said with a smile.

GIVE ME A 168!

Then, just as I was getting hopeful that this Tabitha Sue thing was our only setback of the day, Katarina came sprinting over, looking like someone had just run over her puppy. "Thees ees the most terrible!"

"What's wrong?"

"My skeert! It has been reeped!"

She held up her skirt to show me a rip the size of Montana.

"Yikes," said Jacqui. "All right, calm down, Katarina. This can be fixed." I saw her scanning the crowd for Mom, who notoriously carried things like sewing supplies in her bag. I'd be surprised if she didn't have an entire sewing machine with her for a day like today. Mom finally emerged from the sea of pom-poms and glitter, holding the ice pack over her head.

"Sorry this took so long," she said, handing it to Tabitha Sue. "You wouldn't believe how many people are already injured. It took me ten minutes just to get to the front of the first-aid-kit line."

"We didn't bring our own ice packs?" asked Jacqui.

"We did, but they didn't hold up as well as I would have liked during the long bus ride. It's too bad—hey, what's wrong with Katarina?"

Mom had just noticed Katarina, sitting with her head in her hands. Katarina looked up at us with a

GIVE ME A
169!

mascara-streaked face. "I feel like eediot! I peeked at string and now look!"

She showed Mom the rip.

"Oh," Mom said.

"We were thinking you probably have some sewing supplies on you. Right, Coach?" asked Jacqui.

"Yes, in fact, I do!" Mom said excitedly. "Katarina, come with me. Guys, we'll be back in a jiff."

"Don't worry, Katarina," said Jared as Katarina moped along. "There's time to sew this back up."

Jacqui looked around for the rest of the team but couldn't find Ian and Matt anywhere. Usually all she had to do was call their names and they would come running, but that tactic didn't really work so well in this super-crowded and loud space.

"Tabitha Sue and Jared, you stay here. Maddy, will you come help me round up the troops?"

We searched on the mats first, in case the boys were practicing last-minute stunts. No luck. Then we looked by the canteen. Still no Ian or Matt. The place was too crowded to find these guys easily, even though they looked more like football players than cheerleaders.

"Maybe we should just go back to our spot and hope they show up?" said Jacqui. She sounded a little

GIVE ME A
170!

frustrated. "We need to keep practicing."

"I know," I said, still looking through the crowd for two muscle-y jocks in blue, white, and red. Then, just as I was about to give up too, I spotted them. In the bleachers, talking to a small group of cheerleaders wearing barely more than bikini tops and short shorts (totally against regulation). And guess who was standing nearby with a smug smile on her face? Of course: Clementine.

Ian was standing in that way dudes like to pose to show off their muscles best: hands clasped in front of him so he could flex his biceps while making it seem that this is just how he always looks. Yeah, right! What was this, some kind of bodybuilder contest?

Matt was giving googly eyes to a pint-size cheerleader with the biggest hair I've ever seen. I couldn't imagine how much hair spray went into her cheer look. Can we say Totally Eighties?

In typical Jacqui style, all she had to do was stand near Matt, and within seconds he turned around. He cleared his throat nervously and started blushing like a girl when he realized she was there.

"Oh, hey, Jacqui," he said, with a little squeak.

"Um, this doesn't really look like practicing to me," Jacqui said with an arched eyebrow. "Unless you're just

GIVE ME A 17!!

practicing your flirting technique."

Just then Clementine walked up to us, put an arm around two of the cheerleaders, and smiled innocently. "I was just introducing the boys to some pals of mine. You know, just being friendly."

Jacqui and I were pretty darn sure that Clementine wasn't trying to do us any favors. It's not like she ever gave those guys the time of day when we were at school (ever since they became Grizzlies). Being friendly? I highly doubted it. Being a nuisance? That was more like it.

"The boys are supposed to be with the rest of the team," I said, more to Ian and Matt than Clementine. "And the last thing we need right now are distractions."

I actually didn't mean to be mean, but I realized how that sounded after it came out of my mouth. Oh well. "Come on, guys, let's go," I said. The sooner we got out of the Clementine Circle of Friends, the better.

"Whoa," said Clementine. "You guys need to chill out. All this stress isn't great before a competition."

Jacqui grabbed Ian and Matt by the hands and started dragging them away. "Thanks for the advice, Clem," she said, as we walked away.

"Those girls were nice!" said Ian as we walked toward the Grizzlies. "What's the big deal?"

GIVE ME A 172!

I could tell that Jacqui was in a zero testosterone tolerance kind of mood. "The deal is," she snapped, "Tabitha Sue is injured and Katarina just had a wardrobe malfunction. We don't need anything else to bring us down. Let's just stick together, focus on what we're here to do today, and win. Okay?"

Ian gulped. "Okay, Cap'n."

Thankfully, by the time we got back to the rest of the team, Tabitha Sue was looking a lot better. "I think the ice pack did the trick," she said. "I'm totally fine to get back in the game."

"Awesome. It doesn't even look bad," I said, examining the light pink bruise on her leg.

The problem was, Mom and Katarina hadn't come back yet. I was getting a little worried. I wanted to make sure we'd have time to run through the routine one last time before it was our turn up. And the morning had been going by so fast. By the time you got through the crowds to walk from one end of the gym to the other, that was, like, ten minutes without even trying.

We decided to take the team—minus Katarina—to the mats again to just work on the stunt sequence. It was a little hard to do without one key stunter, but we made it through. Yay! And I was just telling the team

GIVE ME A
173!

to remember their cheer faces (huge, ridiculous grins and eyes on the crowd) when I spotted some familiar faces hovering nearby. It was Lanie, with Marc and even EVAN in tow! My cheer face must have been off the hook, because I just felt like bursting out in song. Finally, after all the nonexistent e-mails, calls, and texts from Evan (and the thousands of e-mails, calls, and texts from MOI), here he was. At my competition.

I ran over to my friends with my arms open wide for hugs. I felt like I was in one of those movies where the sappy music starts playing and the actors run to each other in slow motion.

"You guys! How in the world did you get here?"

Lanie smiled and looked at Evan, who was staring at his shoes. "Don't look at me," said Lanie. "It was all this guy." She jabbed her index finger in Evan's shoulder. "He promised his mom he'd mow the lawn all summer and build a compost heap if she drove us here."

Evan grinned sheepishly up at me. "I'm gonna be elbow-deep in trash and worm poo, that's for sure."

I was so relieved to (a) see Evan here and (b) have him talk to me, I felt like I had wings on my back that were lifting me off the ground.

I realized at that moment just how much the fear of possibly having messed things up with him had been

GIVE ME A 174!

weighing me down. I didn't know what to make of him being here—and whether that meant all was forgiven—but I took it as at least a step in the right direction.

I gave my friends the brief lowdown on the situation—the fact that Clem was here, Tabitha Sue's injury, Katarina's wardrobe malfunction. Evan was laughing along but still wasn't giving me his usual "Maddy is awesome" stare, though. I could tell he was trying to act like the cool guy. He barely looked me in the eye the entire time I told my story, and sometimes he was even looking around the gym like he wasn't really paying attention to what I was saying.

In other words, we were still universes away from how things were just over a week ago. I really tried to not be disappointed and hurt by how he was acting, but it was super hard. A part of me was like, "Why did he come if he was gonna bring this bucket of attitude?" and the other part of me was like, "At least he came! You should be grateful!"

Just then I saw Mom approaching us, with Katarina hot on her heels. Katarina looked like she'd added another layer of makeup to hide the streaks of tears from before.

"It's all fixed!" Mom said proudly. "Just took a little extra time because we couldn't find matching thread."

GIVE ME A
175!

"Tank you very maches, Coach!" said Katarina. She looked at me. "Soon we are going?"

I glanced at my watch. "Any minute now," I said. "Guys! Let's head backstage."

We all started heading over, but Mom just stood there, scanning the crowd. "Hey, Maddy, do you know if Coach Whipley dropped the iPod off at the music booth?"

I was like, "Coach Whipley? Music booth? Huh?"

Mom explained that since she had to attend to Katarina, she had asked Coach Whipley to give our cheer music to the DJ. But I hadn't even seen Coach Whipley leave the bleachers where she'd been sitting and scowling at us the entire time.

I DID realize, however, that Clementine had been mysteriously absent since we'd left her with her cheerleader friends from that other school. This was not sounding good.

We waited for Mom to chat with Coach Whipley, and after a few moments, she came bouncing back with her thumbs up. "We're all ready to go. The music is with the booth guy."

"Well," said Jacqui, "at least there weren't any difficult instructions to follow. There was only one playlist on my iPod, and it was called 'Get Up and

GIVE ME A
176!

cheer! Music," so it should be a no-brainer to the music guy."

Once we were backstage, we brought the team into a group huddle and pumped them up one last time before it was our turn through the curtains closing off the mat. The REAL mat.

"Y'all ready to shred this mat up?" Jacqui asked.

"Yeah," the Grizzlies shouted.

"I can't hear you!"

"Yeah," they said. And then louder the next time: "Yeah! Woooooo!"

"Remember, guys, shoulders down, chins up," I said.

"And no pom-poms below the waist!" said Jacqui.

Mom came running toward us with a can of hair spray. "Wait! Ladies, just a quick spray. Sorry, but we can't have any flyaways on the mat!" She let loose with a cloud of spray so thick we were all coughing as we stretched out our arms and hamstrings one more time.

I was SO NERVOUS. This was the day we'd all been waiting for practically forever, and the moment was finally here. I looked at the rest of the team and saw that everyone had that jittery-slash-fire-in-their-eyes look to them. Finally, we heard the announcer come in over the mic.

GIVE ME A
177!

"And now, from Port Angeles, give it up for the Grizzlieeeeees!"

We all started screaming and ran onto the mat, cheering our heads off until our music started up. Or what we THOUGHT was our music. It actually started off normally. The first counts were just as they always were. We did our beginning stunts with all the hard tumbling and jumps. Then something SERIOUSLY AWFUL happened. I was in the middle of pulling one of my tucks when the music changed from our cheer mix to something by Lil Wayne. I suddenly panicked, wondering if all this time I hadn't been paying attention to our music and just now was realizing that the mix had included this song the whole time. Or maybe I blanked out Jacqui having told us she added it at the last minute. I almost ate the mat, but pulled it together at the last second, making a clean landing, thank goodness. I continued to hit all my motions, until the music changed again. It sounded like a country song that was being played backward, with screeching frogs dubbed over it.

Or at least that's what it sounded like to me. We all tried to just go along with the rest of the routine, and I prayed that the rest of the Grizzlies were watching Jacqui and me so they could keep up with the count.

GIVE ME A 178!

But eventually, we all started losing it one by one like fallen soldiers on a battlefield. Tabitha Sue was the first to turn to me and say, "I can't do this! I'm sorry!" before running off the mat. The rest of the team soon followed, leaving just Jacqui and me doing cartwheels across the mat with smiles plastered on our faces.

"We seem to be having some, uh, technical difficulties," said the announcer. "We're, uh, we're going to, um, hold on just a minute—"

Finally the music went off. The whole auditorium went up in a roar of gasps and shrieks (and of course, a few snickers). I have never heard of anything like this happening during a competition.

Jacqui looked at me like, "Let's get out of here."

I couldn't have run any faster.

When we got backstage, I saw Mom looking completely horrified, as the team practically clung to her side. Her usually rosy cheeks were stark white. I felt like throwing up.

"What happened?" asked Jared, to no one in particular. His hands were shaking.

Mom put an arm around me. "I don't know what half the stuff you guys dance to is. But in all our practice sessions, I know for a fact that we've never cheered to anything like that."

GIVE ME A
179!

Jacqui, for the first time in history, had tears in her eyes. "I'm so sorry, guys. I don't know what to say. But that wasn't my playlist!"

"What WAS that playlist anyway? I've never even heard that last song in my life," said Tabitha Sue.

Jacqui shook her head, wiping her eyes with the back of her hand. "No idea. I uploaded the final mix last week and never changed it. I checked it every night! And even just the other day, I erased every other playlist on my iPod, so that's the only one that could have been there!"

She looked like she was going to start hyperventilating. Mom started making circular motions with her hand on Jacqui's back to help calm her down, like she always did for me when I was little.

"You have to believe me," said Jacqui more steadily. "That was NOT our playlist."

Mom bent down to Jacqui's height, holding her by the shoulders. "Listen, I'm going to go talk to the judges and explain the situation. I'll see if we can have a do-over."

Jacqui crossed her arms over her chest and started walking away from the group. This was BAD.

"Jacqui," I said. "We all know this wasn't your fault."

She just stared down at her sneakers, sniffling.

GIVE ME A
180!

Then the rest of the team came over to her to say that they believed her. "Jacqui, you're, like, the most together person on the whole team," said Matt. "We know you of all people wouldn't mess up something like this."

"Yeah, no one thinks this is your fault," said Ian.

Jacqui smiled. "You know what? If we do get a do-over, the good news is, I borrowed my mom's iPod mini and uploaded the playlist there as a backup." I could see the clouds over Jacqui's head begin to literally part. She wasn't happy unless she was coming up with solutions, so I know these past few minutes had been utterly horrifying to her.

The whole competition seemed to grind to a halt as we huddled backstage, wondering how this had happened in the first place. I knew we needed to talk to Coach Whipley. I had a suspicion that she wasn't the one to switch iPods on us. She was mean, but she wasn't cruel. I snuck around to the bleacher area and saw Evan, Marc, and Lanie talking nervously with one another. I knew they must all have been freaking out for us, but I didn't have the time just then to explain what was going on.

Then my eyes landed on Clementine. She was sitting by herself, her legs crossed daintily, with a big smile on

GIVE ME A 18!!

her face. And she seemed to be laughing into her cell phone, like whoever was on the other end was in on a joke with her.

It was like I'd been punched in the stomach. Could Clementine have taken things THIS far? Was she so out to get me that she would sabotage our competition? Even I had a hard time swallowing the idea. But I had a feeling that whether or not I liked it, it just had to have been her.

When I got back to the rest of the team, Mom was already there, grinning proudly.

"Good news!" she said. "I got you a do-over. You'll be last at the competition, but at least they're giving you a second chance!"

Everyone gave each other a round of high fives. I was happy, but also worried about what this might have done to everyone's confidence level.

"It's still so unfair," said Jacqui, in untypical Jacqui fashion. She always was the one to look on the bright side, so this was REALLY BAD. "We busted our pom-poms for this. And the whole mix thing totally wasn't our fault. Something really smells fishy about this."

I wanted to say, "You can say that again. And by the way, if you're looking for a stinky fish, take a whiff of Clementine over there." But I kept it to myself. If

GIVE ME A 182!

I brought it up now, it would only distract the rest of the team, and besides, I had zero proof anyway.

We made our way back to the bleachers, where Coach Whipley and Clementine were chatting. Coach Whipley got up to talk to us Grizzlies and, I guess, offer her condolences. "In all my years," she said, shaking her head, "I've never seen something like that happen."

"Coach?" I asked. "Are you sure you had the right iPod when you handed it to the music guy?" I knew it took a lot of nerve for me to question Coach Whipley, and that there was a strong possibility that as payback she'd stick me in a locker and leave me to die at some point in the future, but I was willing to take my chances.

Coach Whipley nodded. "Definitely. I got it right from Coach Caroline. Then I had to run to the little girls' room, so I asked Clementine over here to do it."

Clementine put on her best sympathetic and shocked face. "I brought it straight over to the booth. I didn't drop it, blow on it, or anything. I swear I held that iPod like it was a rare baby bird. Are you sure it hadn't been messed with before?" Now she was looking at Jacqui.

Jacqui knows what Clem is capable of, so she must have put two and two together as soon as we found

GIVE ME A 183!

out it was Clem who delivered the music. But she held herself back from doing anything drastic, and I could hear her doing those breathing exercises she always tells me to do when she can tell I'm about to lose it.

"Jacqui," I said in a whisper. "Let's deal with this later, okay?"

She just stared at Clementine, nodding.

"All right," she shouted to the team. "Let's get ready for this do-over."

As soon as the words left her lips, I saw Clementine's smile falter. She obviously hadn't expected us to get another chance. As we walked away from the bleachers, I could hear her talking earnestly to Coach Whipley. I can't say for sure, but I thought I heard the words "unfair advantage" float our way. What is it to her anyway? It's not like she's competing.

I suggested to the rest of the team that we take a little breather and grab some refreshments before starting up practicing again. Everyone was still a little shaken by what had just happened. I mean, it was completely HUMILIATING, especially since no one else knew the situation. For all anyone in the crowd knew, we didn't even know our own music. Or we weren't capable of making a playlist correctly. Even though none of this was our fault, I felt like the co-captain of the

GIVE ME A 184!

Big Loser Squad. I wondered what Evan and Lanie were thinking, and hoped that Evan didn't think I'd looked like a complete clown out there as I danced to the wrong music. None of these thoughts were helping. BAD THOUGHTS, MADISON, BAD! And I couldn't let the team think about stuff like that either. We had to use the time from now until the end of the competition to chill out, then practice.

After everyone had gotten a snack we ran through the routine a bunch of times on the practice mat. Other teams were nice enough to clear a big space for us. That was kind of cool. I guess we were somewhat celebrities. Yay! (Not.)

Even Ian and Matt's "new cheerleader friends" were cheering us on from the sidelines. But miracle of all miracles, the guys didn't seem to even notice. It was kind of funny, actually—the girls kept smiling at the two of them and calling their names, but the boys didn't blink. Not once. I think the fact that something had almost ruined our chances at the competition made them want to be better than ever and show people they couldn't be defeated. Thank goodness for that old football spirit!

When we'd finally hit all our stunts and gotten to a point where we felt like we were in good shape, Jacqui

GIVE ME A 185!

told the team we were ready. "Let's just relax and watch some of the other teams from now until we have to go. You don't want to overdo it, especially since we were ALREADY giving our all out there before."

One of the key secrets for competition day is to give 99% in all your practices, but never 100. You want to save the 100 for the big moment. Jacqui and I were big believers in that.

When I had a moment, I went over to Lanes and the gang.

"Whoa. We've been dying to talk to you!" said Lanie. "What happened?"

Evan was biting his lip with worry. "Are you okay?" he asked.

I nodded. "Yeah. It's kind of a long story. I think I know what happened, but I need some more proof." I brought everyone in close so no one else could hear us. "I think Clementine switched iPods at the last minute. But of course she's claiming innocence."

"Why am I so not surprised?" said Lanie, sharing a look with Marc. I had a good audience, at least. None of them were big Clementine fans.

"Is there anything you want us to do?" said Evan. SO CUTE! My hero.

"No, but thanks," I said. "I mean, I'll figure this out.

GIVE ME A 186!

In the meantime, just scream your heads off when we're up."

"You got it," said Lanie.

Before we knew it, it was our turn again. I could feel the anticipation building in the rest of the gym. Everyone knew it was all or nothing for us at this point. If we flopped, it would be all on us. Clementine and Coach Whipley had made their way backstage, and boy, did Clem not look like a happy camper. It was like the fact that we were going again was causing her physical pain.

Even cold, mean Coach Whipley was trying to cheer Clementine up. Like she deserved that!

The announcer called us onto the mat, and the entire gym started cheering for us. It was hard to hear ourselves over the roar of the crowd. Guess everyone likes an underdog, right? Our music came on—the RIGHT music—and we started again with our opening sequence. I glanced quickly at my teammates and was so relieved to see utter determination on their faces. We were all in the ZONE. Like the ceiling could cave in and it could start raining Skittles and we'd still be cheering like our lives depended on it. Which it kind of felt like they did.

By the time we hit our final pose, with everyone in

GIVE ME A
187!

high Vs, the crowd was losing it. We were all breathing like we'd run the marathon of our lives. Everyone was screaming our name. It was like my wildest fantasy come true!

When we ran backstage, Mom was practically in tears. But for a good reason this time! "I'm so proud of you guys!" she said, opening her arms for a giant group hug.

Coach Whipley congratulated us too. And I think she actually meant it!

I'd never felt this good about one of our routines. We'd totally nailed it! One look at my team's faces and I could tell everyone felt the same way.

We packed up quickly so we could leave as soon as the winners were announced. I didn't expect us to get the highest marks, since I thought it would be hard for the judges to forget our giant flop the first time. So I was completely stunned when we received our scores, but still, I wasn't sure what that would mean in the end.

BUT GET THIS: We actually won SECOND PLACE!!! When the announcement was made, Lanie, Evan, and Marc came running over to congratulate us. I almost missed hearing who won the whole competition because we were so excited about our own win. We were jumping up and down and screaming. Even Ian and Matt got into it! The Hornets won first place. They'd

GIVE ME A 188!

done an amazing job, as I'd expected they would. They hit their routine without any mistakes. It was almost a no-brainer that they'd win.

"Come on, guys!" said Mom. "Let's all celebrate! Hamburgers for everyone!"

I started salivating at the word "hamburger." I hadn't been hungry all day because of my nerves, but all of a sudden dinner sounded like the best idea in the entire world.

On our way out of the gym, Evan came up to me. "I didn't get to give you a congratulatory hug."

He reached his arms around me and hugged me for what seemed like a long time. I wondered if he could feel how fast my heart was beating. I also wondered what this hug meant. We didn't get to sit next to each other at dinner, so there wasn't really that much of an opportunity to figure out where we stood with each other. Oh well.

It was so funny, at dinner, Clementine was totally the odd person out. Our whole team was smushed together at one end of the table, leaving her alone with Coach Whipley and Mom. (Super fun, right? Ha. I actually felt worse for Mom.) Clem basically stayed glued to her BlackBerry the entire time and barely ate anything. I tried not to pay too much attention to what she was up

GIVE ME A
189!

to, because she is so not worth it.

The rest of us Grizzlies, however, had already become suspicious of Clementine. I don't blame them. How could they not? She was the last person who had the iPod in her hands. I think the only person who thought Clem was innocent was maybe Coach Whipley, but I couldn't be too sure. Throughout dinner, people started coming up with pranks that we should play on her. Even sweet Tabitha Sue! At one point she whispered to me that maybe we should loosen the saltshaker and then pass it down to Clementine.

"Tabitha Sue! I'm surprised at you!" I joked.

She smiled. "It seems to always work on TV."

"Trust me, I'm tempted, but I don't need to give her any more reason to do something worse. Not like I can imagine how she CAN do worse, but Clem never stops amazing me."

"Fine, then let's just ignore her for the rest of the night."

"That's easy," I said. "I have zero interest in being nice to her. She can get a taste of what it's like to be the outcast."

When we got on the bus to go home, Lanie and Marc sat next to each other (surprise, surprise), and then Lanie said to Evan and me, "You guys should sit across

GIVE ME A 190!

from us so we can chat." I LOVE LANIE. If she hadn't said that, it would have been total Awkward Town to ask Evan to sit next to me.

But here's the big problem: Even though Evan came out today to support me, and even though he gave me that never-ending hug, here we are sitting next to each other and he's barely talking to me. I'm trying to hide my journal as I write this, and trying not to be hurt or annoyed. But I'm really confused. Is he still mad about the picture? And if he is, why isn't he saying anything? I've been trying to talk to him every chance I get, so he knows that I want to. Just now I even tried to start a convo with him by saying, "So, what's new?" And he was just like, "Yeah, I gotta work on some SuperBoy stuff before the fair tomorrow." So what could I say? Oof! Our knees were just touching, but he moved his away ☹.

THAT NIGHT, POLISHING MY CHEER MEDAL!

We got home kinda late, but I felt like unpacking my cheer bag to give myself a feeling like this was final, the competition was finally over, and now it is time to CHILL.

So anyhoo, as I was unpacking and simultaneously stroking the medal that I was still wearing around my

GIVE ME A 191!

neck, I heard the doorbell ring. I didn't really think much of it—figuring it was probably Mr. D coming by to hang with Mom, but next thing I knew Mom was calling for me.

"Madington! Come downstairs!"

Her voice was a little hoarse from trying to yell above the crowds that day.

A big part of me was hoping, hoping, hoping it was Evan, but as I walked down the stairs, I caught a familiar blond ponytail swish by on its way into the kitchen. Katie?

"You girls want some sundaes?" Mom asked, her head already deep in the freezer.

Katie saw me in the doorway and came running at me with her arms outstretched. "Congrats on the big win!" she said.

"Thanks!" I said, getting a big whiff of her fruity shampoo.

Katie pulled out a chair from our kitchen table and made herself at home. "I heard about the music mix-up," she said, her eyes wide. "But you guys must have really knocked the judges' socks off to make such a comeback!"

"Yeah, it was kind of a miracle," I said, joining her at the table.

Mom laid out three different kinds of ice cream,

GIVE ME A 192!

plus chocolate syrup and sprinkles, all on the counter. "I'm gonna go make some phone calls. You girls enjoy."

"Thanks, Coach!" I said, as she made her way up the stairs.

We each assembled a rockin' good sundae, then sat back down. I was quiet for a while, and Katie must have noticed, because she asked me what was wrong.

I took a big bite of whipped cream, and then came out with it:

"I really hate to say this, because I know how you feel about her, but I'm convinced the music mix-up wasn't really an accident. I think Clem did it."

There, I said it. It was out there, whether I liked it or not. I never stopped feeling awkward about pointing fingers at Katie's best friend, and Katie doesn't make it much easier for me. She always clams up when I bring up the subject, and this time was no different. Besides, I feel like we've had this talk a million times already, and I never get anywhere.

Katie pursed her lips and started picking at the sprinkles on her sundae with her fingers.

"Do other people think that?" she asked finally.

I nodded. "I just feel like I've been keeping so many secrets lately, all so that no one knows about your audition in New York, and it has gotten beyond out of

GIVE ME A
193!

hand, you know? Like, I can't tell Evan about Luc, so now he's practically not talking to me. And we almost lost everything we'd been working for today because Clem never tires of her super Mean Girl act."

Katie nodded but didn't look at me.

"I keep thinking about what you said last time," I continued. "About what her reason is for being like this to me. We still haven't figured out what it could be."

"All right," said Katie. "I have an idea that's been kind of creeping up on me, but I didn't want to admit. What if Clem figured out that I auditioned in New York, and she's mad at me for lying? And maybe she knows somehow that you know, and so she knows we're friends, and she's trying to punish me by hurting you?"

I hadn't even thought about that until Katie said it, but as soon as she did, it made so much sense. Why else would Clem keep upping the ante in her Ruin Maddy's Life campaign?

"Punish you?" I asked. "Why wouldn't she just tell you she knows?"

Katie took a tiny bite of her ice cream. I was kind of losing my appetite too.

"She wouldn't just come out and tell me, because if she felt that I had betrayed her, she would want to teach me a lesson. That's her style. And now I'm not only

GIVE ME A 194!

worried that Clem somehow knows about our friendship and New York, but that she might tell the rest of the team." Katie was getting a little more frantic now. "And if she tells the team, they'll probably be really mad at me. I know Clem. She could make the whole team turn against me if she wanted to. And if that happens, they could try to take captain away from me."

"Really?" I asked, shocked. "They could do that?"

Katie nodded solemnly. "Yeah. If they can argue that my trying out for the dance school shows that I'm not as devoted to the team as I say I am, then they absolutely could do that. And Coach Whipley would definitely agree. She's all about loyalty."

"So basically she keeps doing all this stuff to me so that you'll try to put a stop to it and tell her everything, like, in my defense?"

"Uh-huh."

I couldn't believe I hadn't thought about this until Katie said it. But her theory made sense. And if she's right, it means this wasn't so much about ME in particular. This was about Katie and Clem all along.

"Katie, I hate to say this, but if you think Clem is really the kind of person who would do all this stuff to hurt you, then I don't think she's as good a friend as you think." In a million years I couldn't imagine Lanie

GIVE ME A
195!

doing anything like this to me. Or Evan even. In fact, I'd been pretty rotten to Evan, and the worst thing he'd done was just not talk to me.

"You don't understand," said Katie.

I didn't know what else to say. I was just glad that I didn't have a friend like Clem. But I felt really bad for Katie.

Before going to bed, I decided to get the whole team on video chat. Everyone was online, luckily. It was hard to hear any one person, because we were all practically still jumping up and down over our win.

"Too bad for poor Diane," said Jared sarcastically. "She missed out on all the fun today."

"Jared, when are you gonna just talk to Diane and end this stupid fight?" demanded Tabitha Sue.

"I don't want to waste my breath," said Jared indignantly.

"Guys!" said Jacqui, putting her face up close to her video screen.

"Ew, hello nostrils!" I joked.

She backed up and held the team's second-place award up to the camera. "Um, hello? Can we focus on how AWESOME we were today?"

Everyone cheered so loudly I had to hold my hands over my ears.

GIVE ME A
196!

"I just wanted to tell you," Jacqui continued, "I'm bringing this to the dunking booth tomorrow. And also, I wrote an e-mail to Mr. Datner about placing it in the trophy area outside the gym and he said yes!"

I wasn't sure if this was just Mr. D's way of being nice to Mom through me, but either way it would be way cool to have a Grizzly trophy out there for all the school to see.

Oh and everything is all set for tomorrow, for Lanie's and my booth. Good thing we prepared ahead of time or else I would have been too DEAD to do anything else tonight. I feel like I could sleep forever. But no rest for the weary! Fair tomorrow, bright and early. Ugh.

Just tried to write to E on chat, because his status said "active," but he didn't write back. Either he's still ignoring me, or he got eaten by a hungry bear.

GIVE ME A
197!

Sunday, May 1

After the (totally un-)fair
(ha-ha, that never gets old!)

Spirit Level:

"Awesome" IS NOT Just the Name of a cheer Move!

Seriously. Long. Day. So many ups and downs. But in the end, lots of ups! Where do I begin? Okay, fine, at the beginning (ha-ha)! This morning Lanes and I got ourselves quite a workout just lugging the boxes of T-shirts from Mom's car to our booth. And it really must be spring, because I was literally sweating by the time we were done. I think with the combo of all that pom-pom waving yesterday and the manual labor of today, my arms might literally quit on me.

Lanie knows me so well, she brought us some cool frozen iced coffee drinks that you can buy in the supermarket. Basically, it's like a gallon of sugar and caffeine. YUM-EE. Before long, I was running in circles with energy. Which is a good thing, as long as you don't think about how badly you're gonna CRASH later. But hey, I was living in the moment. Or at least trying to.

GIVE ME A
198!

Evan walked by as we were setting up our booth and barely gave us a wave. Or if I'm being totally honest here, he basically waved at Lanie and didn't really look at me. Nice.

I buried my head in my hands. "He's still mad at me," I said to Lanie.

She put a hand on my back. "I promise you, this thing with Evan will blow over soon."

"He still hasn't said anything to you, has he?" I was kinda hoping maybe they'd talked about things on their ride to the competition yesterday.

Lanie shook her head. "Sorry. But listen, this isn't going to be a morning of Evan and Maddy drama. Right NOW we have to get this booth in order before the crowds stampede us."

"I know, I know," I said. I started posting the different design options on the bulletin board behind us. I have to admit, they looked really cool.

Clementine was running back and forth all over the place, shouting orders into her megaphone. It hit me at that moment that Head Fair Leader wasn't such a stretch for Clem. She's used to shouting things in her megaphone—except in cheer, they're usually inspiring and uplifting things, not orders. She had one poor kid practically shaking with fear. He was bent on

GIVE ME A 199!

the ground picking up a granola bar wrapper that he'd tried to throw into the garbage, but missed by a few centimeters.

"Did I say you should ADD trash to the ground?" she barked. "No, I didn't think so!"

It was only a little bit funny, the way she insisted on using the megaphone even when she was within a foot of whoever she was yelling at.

Thank goodness we'd finished setting up when we did, because literally two seconds later, the school started letting people in. It was mostly parents of students at first, and then a few little kids. A bunch of our friends stopped by to say hi, but no one wanted to make a T-shirt. Guess they wanted to see what else there was out there first! Finally, Mom and Mr. Datner stopped by. Yay! Our first real customers. Trying not to feel like a loser about that.

"Want to design a T-shirt?" I asked Mom.

"Of course, sweetie!" said Mom, perusing the different design options.

Mr. Datner chose an extra-large T-shirt and asked to keep it simple. Since it is kind of hard to get very creative with a guy's T-shirt look, we stuck to just using a decal instead of slashing it up. I couldn't really see Mr. D rocking the heavy metal look.

GIVE ME A 200!

For Mom, we made a cute halter-style shirt. Lanie wanted to make it cropped, too, but I quickly nixed that.

"These are wonderful, Maddy!" Mom exclaimed, holding hers up for Mr. Datner to admire. "Let's put them on now! We can match!"

"Fine. Be just a little more obvious that you're a couple," I muttered.

"What was that?" asked Mom.

I plastered an easygoing smile onto my face. "I said, glad you walked away with a couple of designs!"

Lanie kicked me under the table.

Guess Mom and Mr. D started a trend, because after we did their T-shirts, people started crowding toward our booth. I almost couldn't believe how popular we'd become all of a sudden. All our friends who'd stopped by earlier just to say hi came back asking for their own T-shirt design. It kind of became this "thing" to be walking around the fair in one of our T-shirts.

After what seemed like five straight hours of chopping, drawing, tying, and safety pinning, I needed a BREAK.

"Maybe we need to start making some ugly T-shirts?" joked Lanie. "I can't stand the hordes!"

"I know!"

GIVE ME A 201!

We took turns taking walks around the fair to scope out the other booths. I'd stopped by earlier at the Grizzly dunking booth, but that was pretty much before the fair had started picking up. Now the booth was crowded with people taking pics with their camera phones of the football team getting doused. I'd never seen such glee in Katarina's face as when she was pressing the big red button that ended up soaking the jocks. Everyone was laughing, most of all their coach.

"Whoo, boys!" he said, clutching his stomach as one kid spouted water out his mouth like a whale. "Hope you're thirsty!"

I caught Jared walking toward the Titan booth a couple of times, and had a feeling he was stalking Diane. Every time he'd get close, he'd just stare in her direction, and then as soon as she turned, he'd skulk away, shaking his head. I still couldn't believe they hadn't made up after all this time.

Which reminded me . . . I wondered how Evan's booth was doing. His was in full swing as well. He had a nice line of people waiting for their own personal SuperBoy comic. It was kind of like those caricatures that you get done at carnivals, but instead of just getting a picture of yourself, it showed YOU inside a scene from

GIVE ME A 202!

a SuperBoy comic. I walked right up to him, where he was scribbling his signature at the bottom of one of his works.

"So I guess you do have a fan club," I said.

Evan smiled at me, and then, as if he was just reminding himself about why he'd been mad at me this whole time, made that smile disappear faster than the Tater Tots in the cafeteria.

"So is your new friend coming to the fair?" he asked, not looking at me as he started in on his next drawing.

I knew he meant Luc. And it was funny he hadn't brought that up at all yesterday at the competition, but maybe he didn't want to get into a fight when I needed to be in competition mode. And even after we'd placed second, he probably didn't want to ruin the celebration with more drama. I guess.

"No. He was just in town for that one day." I did my best not to sound like I was defending myself.

"In town from where?"

"New York." I hoped that if he knew Luc was all the way from New York, he'd stop worrying about this already. Then I realized that telling him this maybe was a bad idea. Because then he'd think that this was someone I'd met during my trip (he'd be right) and

GIVE ME A
203!

that I had a crush on (he'd be wrong).

When I saw Evan's frown deepen, I quickly backpedaled. "But I swear, it really isn't what it seems like." Even I could hear how lame I sounded. Gaaaah! SO frustrating.

Finally he put his pen down and looked at me. "Look, I'm pretty busy fighting off the hordes, so . . . talk to you later?"

"Yeah, sure."

I couldn't believe it! By opening my big fat mouth, I'd only made things **WORSE**!

I sulked back to my booth. "What, did the Grizzlies try to dunk you or something?" asked Lanie.

"No, but Evan did. In his own way."

"Oh Mads . . ."

"Come on, distract me. Let's straighten up here a bit or something."

Katie came by while we were freshening up the booth. "The Titan booth is totally deadski. It's like a ghost town."

"Seriously?" I asked. "I'd have thought that with a fancy stylist person like Clementine's mom, they'd be pushing people away."

"I think people are afraid of Mrs. Prescott, actually," Katie whispered. "The first few people who

GIVE ME A 204!

came for their style evaluation nearly walked away in tears!"

"I guess the apple doesn't fall far from the tree, does it?" quipped Lanie.

Katie stuck around to learn how to slash a T-shirt in a cute and fashionable way, and I showed her how to make hers have a bunch of slits in the back. Of course when she put it on, it looked like she'd invented the whole look herself. Katie's just special like that.

"Hey Maddy," said Katie, gathering her T-shirt scraps into her palm. "You okay? You look upset."

I'm not so good at hiding my emotions.

"Well, I tried talking to Evan for the millionth time, and he basically told me to get lost."

"He's still mad about the picture?"

Lanie nodded yes for me. "Oh yeah."

Katie took a deep breath and got up from her chair. "Okay. I've decided this is just too much. Enough is enough. I can't be the reason that your love life gets ruined. I'm talking to Clem now."

"Really?" I practically squeaked. I'd been waiting for her to say those words for, like, ever. I wasn't sure if my ears were hearing right.

"Yeah. I'm tired of wondering why she's acting this

GIVE ME A 205!

way, and being afraid of her doing something even worse."

"Wow," I said. "Thanks, Katie. That means a lot. Want me to go with you?"

"Actually, yeah," she said. "That would be nice. Then after, we can all explain to Evan what that picture really was about."

Lanes said she'd man our booth while I stepped away. "Report back to me on everything!" she said. "Don't spare me one detail!"

But just as we got up to the Titan booth, we saw the entire team looking on awkwardly as Clementine and her mom had a shouting match. I hadn't really taken a good look at her mom before, but I could see where Clementine got all her good looks from, AND her attitude. Her mom had perfectly windblown hair, smooth caramel-colored skin, huge eyes, and big pouty lips. She was wearing a fitted blazer, dark, flared jeans, mile-high heels, and one of those alligator-skin bags that probably cost more than my house.

Her mom had her finger pointed directly at Clementine's face. "Clem, did you see how much traffic that other booth was getting? Those girls and their stupid T-shirts? Get your act together and make this booth a success, or else. I mean it." Then she turned on her heels and sashayed away, clicking open her phone

GIVE ME A 206!

and talking hurriedly to whoever was on the line.

Sheesh. I couldn't believe she was jealous of MY booth.

"But Mom!" Clementine pleaded. "It's not my fault! They're closer to the entrance! That's why everyone is going there first!" Her mom didn't even flinch. For a second I saw Clementine's usual confidence falter, and I almost thought she was going to cry. She slunk into her chair and took out her phone. It was definitely one of those moves to show that she was just too busy replying to all her text messages to care that her mom had just yelled at her in front of everyone.

The other Titans had started pretending they were too involved in their own conversations to have noticed what just happened between Clem and her mom. So embarrassing. I mean, I have to deal with my mom dating my gym teacher, but at least she would never embarrass me by yelling at me in front of my friends or my teammates.

I looked at Katie and could tell she was concerned. "Listen, Katie, maybe we should come back later. She seems pretty riled up."

"Maybe you're right," Katie agreed. "See what I mean, though, about the way her mom treats her?"

"Yeah, I do."

GIVE ME A 207!

It was definitely the "right" thing to do, but then again, did Clementine deserve us being so nice? We'd started to turn around and walk away, when Clementine spotted us.

"Excuse me, but where do you think you're going?" she asked, matching our strides.

"Keep walking," Katie whispered to me. Then she turned to talk to Clem. "It's not a big deal. We're just walking back to Madison's booth to check it out."

Clementine followed us to the booth. We tried to ignore her, but when we got to the booth, she walked right up to it, looking like she was about to burst with anger. I had a feeling, just by the look in her eye, that whatever was about to come out of her mouth wasn't going to be pretty. "Ha," she said, pounding one fist loudly on our table. Her gaze fell on the T-shirt Katie was wearing. "Well, well. Looks like you ALREADY went to the dark side to check out their booth." She picked up the edge of Katie's shirt, and then dropped it, as if it were dripping with cooties. "Oh, Katie. Didn't anyone tell you that the homeless look is so last year?"

Katie didn't laugh.

"Oh, come on. Can't you take a joke? Aren't I hilarious?"

"Ha-ha," said Lanie. "Can't you leave now?"

GIVE ME A
208!

"No," said Clem. "I am the Head Fair Leader, and it is my job to make sure things are running smoothly. And in my position, I believe that this booth just isn't going to work."

"What?" I asked.

Clementine looked at her watch, as if she had a kind of Mean Girl Alarm. "You guys have to close down immediately."

At this point, a bunch of Titans had already made their way toward all the commotion. If there's one thing cheerleaders like, it's a smackdown-style confrontation.

"For what reason?" said Lanie.

"I don't need a reason. This is simply my call." Obviously her quick fix to not getting enough visitors to her booth was to CLOSE ours. Before anyone could stop her, she started collecting our piles of T-shirts and taking the tacks and our designs down. "Katie, would you help me out here?" she said.

Katie didn't budge.

"Hello? Earth to Katie. I'm TALKING to you."

Finally, Katie struck back. "No, Clementine. I'm not one of your minions! And you've taken things too far."

Clementine pointed one of her perfectly manicured fingers in my direction. "Oh, so you're defending Miss Grizzly over here?"

GIVE ME A 209!

"Yes," said Katie, a little hesitantly. "She's my . . . friend."

Clem suddenly got this look on her face that screamed "gotcha." "Aha! So you admit it. You ARE friends. What, were you too embarrassed to say it before? What ELSE do you want to admit to?" she said, narrowing her eyes at Katie. But she didn't wait for a response. "Maybe you have some jazz shoes you want to tell me and the Titans about?"

Uh-oh.

"Clementine," said Katie in a harsh whisper. "Please let's not talk about this here." She grabbed Clem by the arm and tried to lead her away, but Clem yanked her arm away.

"It seems like you've been keeping a lot of secrets from me lately. Secrets from your best friend. Or should we say FORMER best friend, since all you ever seem to do lately is meet with HER in your secret meeting places?"

It sounded like Clem was about to cry. Her voice was cracking a little, and her face had started to contort into a grimace. "I know everything," she continued. "I followed you guys one day and listened from inside a closet in the classroom."

Katie gasped. "You WHAT?"

GIVE ME A 210!

"I heard about your little audition. Why didn't you tell me?"

Clem now had tears in her eyes. Behind her, the Titans were tittering and whispering to one another.

Katie must have realized the time to speak was now, because it didn't seem like Clementine's tirade was going to end anytime soon. "Okay, let me explain," she said, looking first at Clementine and then at the rest of her teammates. "I thought you and the Titans would never talk to me again if you knew," she said softly. "So I didn't tell you when I went to New York for the audition. And then I wanted to tell you, but the longer I kept it a secret, the worse I thought you'd react. And maybe you'd all want to take away my title as captain."

Clementine shook her head. "Maybe some of our teammates would have been mad about it, but I would have put them in their place. I'd never take away captain from you. You're my best friend. My only real friend. I tell you all my secrets. I just can't believe you didn't trust me with the same. It seems like the only one you trust your secrets to is Madison."

Katie's face filled with regret. I'm sure she felt bad about not having confidence in her friendship with Clementine.

I was completely shocked at where this

GIVE ME A
2!!!

conversation was going. I'd never seen Clementine so vulnerable. And also, Katie had pretty much been right on the money about this all along.

"So you switched the music at the competition, and you sent that picture of me and Luc to Evan?" I asked.

Clementine nodded.

"Why?" asked Katie.

"I wanted to get you to defend Maddy, so I could hear you admit that you guys are friends, and everything else you were hiding from me. Especially about your audition."

"Guess I'm more selfish than you thought," said Katie sadly. "I didn't defend Maddy at all." She turned to face me. "I'm really sorry for dragging you into this and not sticking up for you sooner." Then she looked at Clementine. "Why didn't you just talk to me about all this?"

Clementine looked at the floor. "I felt you drifting away, I guess, even before you left for New York. I couldn't stand the idea of losing my best friend."

Nearby, Hilary let out an angry huff.

"Oh, get over it, Hilary!" snapped Clementine. "Katie, you're the only person who really gets me. The only one I've ever trusted and thought wouldn't hurt me. But I might have taken things a little too far."

GIVE ME A
212!

If there were sad violins playing, I wouldn't have been surprised.

I know, I know, it is not nice of me to not feel sorry for Clementine, but it is hard to get over all the horrible things she's done to me. Even if it was all because she was scared of losing her BFF.

I looked over at Katie and saw that now SHE had tears in her eyes. This was turning into an all-out sob fest!

"Oh Clem, I'm sorry for not trusting you. I know you care about me. It's just that sometimes, you're kind of good at hiding it. So I started thinking you'd become this person who would walk all over people just to get what you wanted—like my captain position. But the truth is, no matter what, you could never lose me." Katie walked up to Clem and grabbed her in a giant hug.

Lanie made quiet barfing noises next to me.

"Awwwww!" All the Titans were looking on at Clem and Katie like this was the cutest thing ever. I mean yeah, it was nice to see that they'd made up, but that didn't exactly change the fact that Clem had almost ruined my life.

Then Clementine surprised me: she asked if she could talk to me alone. (That part isn't so surprising, because what she was about to do probably would have

GIVE ME A
213!

sent her Mean Girl reputation into oblivion. I'm sure she figured that she'd already shown the world her soft side enough today.) When we were out of hearing range, she actually apologized to me for what she'd done with the booth stuff, and the picture thing. I should have had a little recorder with me, because the day that Clem owned up to her actions and apologized to me should forever be remembered. It's one thing to hear Clem say nice things to her best friend. Another for her to say them to ME. I have a feeling it won't happen again anytime soon.

"I was really jealous of your friendship with Katie," she said. "And I couldn't believe Katie wouldn't tell me about her audition, but instead told you. I know I took it out on the wrong person."

Then she was like, "But if you tell anyone else I said that, I'll completely deny it. And just WHO do you think people will believe?"

Yeah, that was more like Clementine. I was beginning to get SCARED. Having Clem turn into this supersweet person from now on would be like Lady Gaga dressing like our school librarian.

"Okay, well, thanks, Clem. I appreciate your apology. But there's one thing you can do for me."

"Yeah?"

GIVE ME A
214!

"You can back me up when I tell Evan that it was you who took that photo and sent it to him. And that there obviously wasn't anything going on between me and Luc—you just made it look that way."

Clem nodded her head in agreement, but I could tell she didn't really like owing me any favors.

Before she could change her mind, I raced over to Evan's booth. Somehow he hadn't moseyed on over with the rest of the world to hear the fight that just went down. Either he was dead set on avoiding me or his booth had been really busy.

"Can we talk?" I asked.

Evan looked up from his sketching to see how many people were waiting for their SuperBoy sketch. Zero. It was almost closing time, after all.

"Okay."

So I told him EVERYTHING. It was like truth-vomit was pouring out of my mouth (gross). I told him how Katie had ended up being in the same hotel I was at when I went with Dad to New York. I told him about her audition and how we ended up kind of bonding. And how she invited me out with her dancer friends and that one of them was this guy Luc. I told him how Luc e-mailed Katie about his coming to Port Angeles and wanting to hang, but that I couldn't tell Evan about it because then I'd have to

GIVE ME A 215!

explain how Katie and I had ended up friends with him. And that Clem was out to get me, so she took a photo that made it look like Luc was, like, my boyfriend or something. When I was finished, Evan just stared at me, like he was computing all these new facts I'd just thrown at him.

"Okay," he said. "So that guy, Luc. He's not, like, your new crush or something?"

"YOU'RE my crush," I said, kind of without thinking.

"I'm sorry, Maddy, for acting so suspicious and weird. I just hate it when you keep things from me."

Wow, he and Clementine had something in common. Secrets were a big no-no. I was glad Evan apologized, but HELLO! Way to keep a girl in suspense. He hadn't really acknowledged what I'd just said to him about him being my crush. I worked up all the courage in my body and just asked him back, "Am I YOUR crush?"

Evan smiled. "Well, I uh . . . was hoping actually that maybe you'd be my girlfriend."

"Duh! Of course I'd like to be your girlfriend." I was smiling so big, I thought my face would break.

So then I sat down next to him at his booth and asked if he'd draw me a SuperBoy comic now that the fans seemed to be taking a breather.

And guess what he drew? A picture of SuperBoy and BestGirl, with BestGirl wearing one of my T-shirt

GIVE ME A
216!

designs, and SuperBoy kissing BestGirl on the cheek!

"Aw, thanks, E. I love it," I said.

THEN, just as I was thinking he'd say something like "You're welcome" or "Glad you like it," he leaned in and kissed me. KISSED ME! Ahhhhh!!!! (Doing crazy hyper dance as I write.) It was for real. As in we were totally official. Maddy and Evan. And for the first time in, like, EVER, seeing our two names side by side like this doesn't seem weird. At all.

He told me we should meet up later and hang, and I definitely agreed. But unforch, I had to get back to Lanie just then in case we had any last-minute customers. Also, I was excited to tell her all about what had just happened.

As I walked away holding his drawing near my heart (because I'm sappy like that), I passed Diane and Jared sitting on the grass and laughing. I gave them a little wave. Seems like school fairs can end fairly. It was the day for people to make up and start over.

GIVE ME A 217!

If you think Maddy's life is full of drama, then wait until you meet Grace, Christina, and the rest of the

Pool Girls

Available at your favorite store!

Published by Simon Spotlight
KIDS.SimonandSchuster.com